MW01148908

One of my favorite chil⎽⎽⎽⎽ ⎽⎽⎽⎽⎽⎽⎽ has always been *Anne of Green Gables*, the heartwarming tale of irrepressible orphan, Anne Shirley, and her adventures living at Green Gables on Prince Edward Island. I started collecting copies of Lucy Maud Montgomery's first novel since the age of ten, and I now own five new copies and two vintage printings. The story itself captivated me—my imagination immediately conjuring up images of the little enchanted green and white cottage that never left me.

I stood in my office, holding one of the vintage copies, thinking about the book I was currently writing. I had stalled in the writing process, feeling like I had little to no inspiration these days. It was summer now, Luke's last summer in Massachusetts before leaving for grad school in Oregon. It had been months since we had even considered exploring—I was still reeling from the "tragic incident."

At home little had changed, although my office now boasted a second desk that was dedicated to a 1950s Smith Corona typewriter that I used for my writing most days. I used my computer only sporadically, as I was still avoiding reading the news or checking my e-mail. For weeks after the fire at Westwood, the Internet had been flooded with stories of Cameron Voegel's death, as well as the arrest of a former explorer, Mike Touchette, who had been charged with starting the fire and was now in jail. The urban exploration forums were inundated with questions and conjectures about the fire, but none of these accounts would ever come close to the truth. Occasionally, I still had nightmares about Westwood, but they were starting to become fewer and far between.

I slid *Anne* back on the shelf and picked up my phone to call Luke. "I know it's rather last minute, but I'm dying for a bit of adventure. Want to find someplace off the grid to photograph?"

"Absolutely. How about that run-down paper mill you mentioned the other day?" Luke asked, the sound of something banging around on the other end of the line. "That place sounds pretty chill."

"Sounds like a plan. Pick me up in ten?"

"Sounds good."

I slid my phone back into my pocket, then put the water on to boil. I took my travel mug down from the cabinet above the sink, so I could have one last cup of tea before we headed out. It didn't matter to me that it was nearly 90 degrees outside. I had to have a cup of tea before I could really get going.

Always late, Luke pulled up to my house fifteen minutes later in his beat-up white Nissan with the black rear bumper. Like me, Luke kept everything he owned in his car—his camera, his bag, his skateboard, sneakers, markers, sketch books. It seemed to me like most creative people kept the objects they loved with them on a daily basis. You never knew when you might find the perfect photo opportunity or an empty swimming pool to skate.

I went downstairs and opened the passenger-side door, picking up a giant CD case that was covered in graffiti and threw it into the overflowing backseat. I kept my camera bag at my feet, as it seemed like the amount of junk in Luke's backseat had multiplied since the last time he picked me up.

We pulled out of my driveway and headed east to the tiny village of Baldwinville. I lived in the town of Pioneer, but portions of the town were split into smaller villages like Baldwinville and nearby Otter River. The Baldwinville Paper Company wasn't much to see and was only marginally photogenic, but it was just what we both needed to get out and feel some inspiration.

"The mill isn't much to see, but it's super quiet and laid back. It'll really only be good for a couple of hours of exploring."

Luke nodded. "Is there anything else in the area that might be worth checking out?"

I thought for a minute, but unfortunately, nothing came to mind. I had been out of the exploring game for a number of months while available locations changed almost daily. "Let me send out a few texts and see if anyone else has any ideas." I scrolled through my list of contacts and sent a few messages, asking for ideas for a nice low-key location.

We pulled into the parking lot behind a dirty-looking Italian restaurant and pulled our gear together. The asphalt in front of the mill was dry and cracked, tall grass was sprouting from almost every inch of mutilated concrete, brown from lack of water, and swaying in the stagnant summer breeze. We walked slowly as there was no reason to rush.

The mill had been empty for years, and I knew almost nothing about it. It was one of the few locations I had checked out frequently, yet I never had the desire to do any research. Inside we prowled around the production floor with our cameras, manipulating shadow and light to get the best texture in each photograph. The glass- block walls on the east side of the building took in the sun and bent the light, throwing it onto the floor in arcs and swirls.

But I quickly grew bored of the same angles, the same lines. The only problem was that I still hadn't received any replies to my text, so at the moment we had nowhere else to go. I packed up my camera and went to sit down on the loading dock to feel the slight breeze that had grown stronger, sweeping through the waist-high weeds.

"Hey, you done?" Luke asked as I flinched. "Sorry, didn't mean to scare you." Sometimes he moved so quietly that he scared the hell out of me without meaning to.

"Yeah. I think I'm all set."

Luke checked his cell phone. "Anyone get back to you with other spots?"

I shook my head, pulling out my own phone. "Well, that could be why. I have no signal in here."

Smirking at me, Luke hopped down from the crumbling dock and turned to hold out his hand to me, helping me down. We headed back through the weeds to the parking lot. As we drew closer to the car, I could feel my phone vibrating repeatedly in my pocket.

"My phone buzzed. Let's hope someone has some ideas for us, or else we're heading home mighty early." I scrolled through my texts, barely glancing at the repeated expressions of blank apology from other explorers who were surprised to hear from me, yet were not very forthcoming with suggestions.

One, however, looked to be a decent possibility.

"How about a house in the next town over?"

With a shrug, Luke agreed that the house was a definite option. "Sounds good. Good and quiet." He smiled. Sometimes he was so difficult to read. Was it too much to ask to show a girl at least a flicker of excitement?

"Hopefully, it'll be interesting." I tossed my camera bag back into the car and pulled out the half-frozen bottle of water I had left in the cup holder. Exploring always left my mouth coated in dust— a strange-tasting dust that, I supposed, could have been somewhat psychological, but the cold water seemed to help wash some of it away.

Luke, too, was knocking back a bottle of water. He finished it off, tossing the empty into his trunk, which seemed to be collecting the junk overflow from the backseat. He walked back around the car, folding himself into the driver's seat. I climbed in after him, anxious to get the air moving through the car before my internal organs began to sizzle in the heat.

We pulled away from the paper mill and onto Route 202 West, following the vague directions I had received in a text from a local explorer. Lines of cool green trees zipped past, dotted occasionally by cow barns and weathered New England farmhouses that lined the perimeter of the Quabbin Reservoir. The manmade body of water had always fascinated me.

It had been filled to capacity in 1946 after the towns of Dana, Enfield, Greenwich, and Prescott were flooded. Although most of the buildings were moved and the residents evacuated, Quabbin still struck me as something of an underwater ghost town. The flooding of the Reservoir was even used as the opening scene of *In Dreams*, a movie starring Robert Downey Jr. and Annette Bening. The rest of the movie was filmed at Northampton State Hospital just twenty minutes south of our current destination.

Driving slowly, Luke and I craned our necks looking for Blackbird Road. The stretch of road we had pulled onto was long, dry, and dusty with clouds rolling up and over the car in hot, golden billows.

"Hey, there it is!" I almost yelled.

Slamming on the brakes, Luke skidded slightly in the sand and then steered the car onto the street that was marked only by a small wooden hand-painted sign. The soft road turned into pavement, and the trees along both sides of Blackbird Road reached across to the other side of the street, as if they were trying to grow into each other. The canopy of leaves created a cooling effect, letting in only the tiniest rays of sunlight. Every twist and turn of the road took us deeper into a wooded hamlet—so deep, in fact, that we did not notice we had driven too far until we passed the house.

"Was that it?" Luke asked, trying to look over his shoulder while navigating the deserted road.

"I think so."

"Did you see a driveway or some place to pull in?"

I shook my head. "We drove by too fast."

Luke swung the car around in a wide U-turn and headed slowly back in the opposite direction. "No driveway, but I think we can pull right onto the lawn." He nosed the car onto the grass and eased it as far back into the yard as possible where the car was concealed by ripe flowering bushes and wild roses.

I climbed out of the car and wandered around to the front of the house where I stopped to stare at the squat little cottage. It was hidden behind green vines and more bushes that were covered in petite pink blossoms. The vines climbed up and over trellises on either side of the wide green front door. Black shuttered windows flanked the front of the house, white curtains still hanging behind the glass. White peeling clapboard completed the picture, reflecting the green glow of the overgrown plant life.

To the right of the main cottage, a small addition looked like it had literally sprouted up from the original house, ending where it connected to a large red barn that leaned precariously toward the street. After a quick peek in the windows, I followed Luke around to the back of the house.

We had to fight our way through the thorns and brambles that had grown out of control. Threaded through the overgrowth were strands of barbed wire, most likely to keep deer out of the gardens. It had grown slack over the years and was now easy to step on and over into the backyard. It all must have been beautiful at one time with blackberry bushes and flowering vines crowding near the back of the house, the grass stretching all the way to the edge of the woods.

"Someone watches this house."

Luke turned to see what I was talking about. "You're right, the lawn has been mowed recently."

"Someone is taking care of this place." I looked around at the neatly trimmed grass, a sharp contrast to the rambling vegetation closer to the house. The person mowing the lawn was most likely a neighbor or friend who was tasked only with mowing, not with taking a machete to the jungle that was creeping toward the house.

"Do you still want to go in?" he asked.

I nodded. "It looks interesting...even more interesting knowing that someone is caring for it even though it's obviously abandoned."

Moving closer to the back of the house, I could see that a window had been covered with flimsy particleboard and was held in place with tiny wood screws. I slid my fingers under the rotting wood and easily lifted it away from the window frame.

Luke pulled a red plastic cooler close to the foundation and stepped up on it, then jumped through the open window. Because I am far less graceful, I climbed onto the cooler, shoved my bag through the window, and struggled inside after it onto a rickety wooden counter lined with daisy patterned Contact paper.

We found ourselves in a small pantry with shelves that were still lined with pots and pans, dishes, cups, and canned food. An ironing board was propped up against the wall and a 1950s-era white and chrome refrigerator was tucked into a corner surrounded by shelves. A closed wooden door on the right side of the room led, presumably, to the kitchen.

[Insert drawing]

"We're losing light. We'll have to move fast." Luke checked the time on his cell phone.

"That's fine. I can't imagine there will be too much to see." That is, unless the rest of the house was miraculously packed as full as the pantry.

Pulling the wooden door open, I held my breath as the rusted hinges screamed in protest. I hated making so much noise, especially when I had no idea what awaited me on the other side of the door. However, the only thing laying in wait was a small, grungy-looking kitchen that had not been updated for at least fifty years.

The stove and sink were white and from the same era as the refrigerator in the pantry. A rectangular, pumpkin-colored Formica-topped table sat under the windows on the left wall that faced the street, the bushes outside creeping through the broken glass and reaching over the kitchen table.

[Insert drawing]

Next to the pantry door, another identical wooden door was partially open in the opposite direction, allowing a glimpse into the living room beyond. I quickly unpacked my camera, the waning light suddenly spurring me into action. We would not have long to move through the house, and I wanted to get as many shots as possible.

Leaving my bag in the kitchen, I pushed the door to the living room fully open but then stopped short when I realized what I was seeing.

"It's full." I shook my head in disbelief as I surveyed the couch, easy chairs, the table with a record player on it, the cushioned window seat, the table lamps, the painting above the fireplace. "Luke, the living room is full!"

He slid up behind me and followed my gaze from the floor-to-ceiling bookcases that were overflowing with volumes of every shape, size, and color. Immediately we both started snapping frame after frame, the only sounds were the shuffle of our tripods and the grinding of the cameras' automatic-focus lenses.

The light continued to fade away, pushing us to move faster so that we could see the rest of the house. When we were finished in the living room, we moved to the closest door between the bookcase and the fireplace, following it into a bedroom. Surprisingly, it was also fully furnished.

[Insert drawing]

Two oak spindle beds were pushed against the nearest wall; a bureau—four drawers painted white—was pushed against the opposite wall. This room had a fireplace of its own, although it was substantially smaller than the one in the living room.

[Insert drawing]

Through a corner door was a small bathroom with a large claw foot tub, peeling wallpaper, and a wooden drying rack still laden with towels now dried stiff. The bottom of the tub was caked in black flakes, and the toilet bowl was ringed with rusty pools of old water. The bathroom led into a convoluted little hallway the size of a cardboard box with doors on all sides. It reminded me of *Alice in Wonderland*—which door to choose?

One door led into a second bedroom; the other led into a sitting room of sorts with boxes strewn across the floor. This room, different from all the others, was dark, and the windows were tightly boarded. The dark blue indoor-outdoor carpet smelled dank and musty. Silverfish crawled in and out of the boxes, and old record albums were piled precariously on every surface.

[Insert drawing]

The room was obviously part of the addition. It sagged almost six inches lower than the threshold, and the cheap construction was a far cry from the solid quality of the other rooms. The floor felt damp and soggy below my feet, certainly not like the wide hardwood planks in the rest of the house.

Another small, oddly placed hallway connected the room to the sun porch I had seen from the front yard. More bookcases were jammed to overflowing in this hallway, and a small potbelly stove sat propped up in a corner. Yet another wooden door led out to the sprawling backyard.

[Insert drawing]

Rather than take photos in the tiny hallway, I stopped to pore over the hardcover books stuffed into the shelves. Volumes of poetry sat snuggled together with science texts and travel guides. Some volumes were in German, others in French, just like in the living room. Whoever lived here had loved to read.

"I'm going upstairs."

"Holy mother of God!" I whirled around, clutching my chest, my heart thundering. "You scared the hell out of me. Again!"

Luke chuckled. "You coming?"

I narrowed my eyes at him. "Sure. Just as soon as my breathing returns to normal."

He was starting to get the idea that sneaking up on me in abandoned buildings was funny.

To get to the stairs, we had to follow the labyrinth of rooms and hallways back to the front of the house, through the living room, and past the front door to the stairs. Before we even ascended, we could feel the heat—ripe with dust and the scent of mold—floating down and wrapping around our bodies.

At the top of the stairs was another bookcase, and to the right of it, a beautiful glass-paned door that led to what appeared to be a bedroom. I went through the glass door first and into what could have only been the master bedroom. A full-size bed, still made up for someone, was pushed against one wall. Side tables with clear-glass lamps flanked the bed; on the other wall was a standing cabinet-style AM radio.

[Insert drawing]

I walked around the entire second floor through each connecting door, through a corner storage room under a steeply pitched roof. A small room, in no man's land, was mired between the storage room and another bathroom. The whole mess then looped back to a second bedroom and ended in a bedroom with a low, angled ceiling. The tiny space had no decoration save a tiny needlepoint of a rocking horse hanging on the wall.

There was no more time for photographs; the light had almost completely dimmed.
"Luke?" I had lost him somewhere along the way. "Luke, we need to get going. The light's almost gone."

"Yeah. Coming."

I could hear him, but it was damned near impossible to figure out where he was exactly. When he appeared at the top of the stairs, we headed toward the first floor kitchen where we had left our bags. We slipped back out through the window, through the bushes, and to the front of the house where I stopped again to look at the cottage in the waning light of early dusk.

"Are you going to post any photos online?" I asked Luke.

"I might. What should I call it?" For a place like this, it was smart to disguise the real name or location since it looked like no one else had touched the house but us. It would be a shame for a place like this to be ruined by other explorers or worse, vandals.

I thought for a moment, staring at the front of the little cottage. "Green Gables. It reminds me of what I always imagined Green Gables would look like."

***

I uploaded the photos I had taken onto my computer and flipped through them slowly. The house looked just as dark and hauntingly beautiful as it had in person— except for one thing.

I picked up my cell phone and called Luke, but his voicemail message replied instead. "Luke, it's Abby. Listen...we have to go back to the house. None of my photos are usable. I must have moved too fast because they're all out of focus. Call me when you get this."

By 9:00 p.m., my eyes were heavy, the heat and humidity made me feel sweaty and lethargic. I drifted off to sleep, dreaming of the never-ending maze of rooms at the cottage I now thought of as Green Gables.

In the morning, the voicemail light was blinking on my cell phone. Luke, a bit of a night owl, had apparently returned my call at 1:00 a.m.

"Hey, Abby. Yeah...I don't know. I wasn't moving fast like you, but my shots are totally out of focus, too. Oh well. Good thing we can get back there easily. How's this weekend? Hit me up."

I sent him a quick text message to tell him that this weekend was fine, then sat down to write for a bit. It was already Thursday, so the weekend would come fast.

It was another blazing-hot day as we found ourselves pulling onto Blackbird Road once again. We parked in the same spot and climbed out of Luke's car.

It was morning this time, and sunlight streamed through the trees and danced over the flowers scattered around the yard. The cottage looked idyllic in the early- morning light. The peeling paint, cracked foundation, and crumbling roof were somehow less obvious in the glaring summer sun.

We entered the same way through the pantry window and onto the wooden counter below. The pantry was dark, in spite of the bright light outside. When we left the last time, I had closed all the doors behind us—a quick and easy way to tell if anyone else had been there in our absence—but the doors were still closed.

Luke opened the door to the kitchen and held it open for me. In the kitchen, shadows danced across the table and spilled onto the floor. I decided to start taking pictures in the living room while Luke stayed in the kitchen. Setting my bag on the floor, I unpacked my camera, wondering where I wanted to start.

The bay window with the rose-colored cushioned seat caught my eye first. The sunlight was coming through the surrounding windows just right, so I could not resist trying to capture the image. My camera rested on my tripod while I connected my remote shutter release, which was necessary to minimize motion and shaking in the photos.

I snapped a few frames while low to the ground in order to test the light and angle; it looked beautiful on the LCD monitor, but my knees were starting to ache from kneeling down. I put the remote on an end table and stood up to stretch my legs and my arms.

Just then I heard the sharp, mechanical clicking of my camera's shutter firing repeatedly. Puzzled, I thought perhaps I had leaned on the remote shutter release, but I noticed it was out of reach on the end table.

The camera was firing on its own.

The sound continued, echoing exceptionally loudly in the small space, and Luke came bursting into the room. "What the hell is that sound?"

"It's my camera. It's firing on its own."

"Are you leaning on the remote?"

I shook my head. "It's doing it all on its own." I moved toward my camera and pressed the shutter button, which typically stopped it from firing. It refused to stop, however, and continued to snap frame after frame. "It won't stop."

Luke seemed glued to the spot, watching my camera operate independently without any human intervention. "Can you turn it off?"

"I guess that's the only thing I can do." I reached over and turned off the camera, counted to ten, and then turned it back on. It was fine, working perfectly. I switched the camera over to display mode and flipped back to where the camera had started to malfunction. It had taken 28 frames in all, but it did not seem like there was anything in them that was visible. "There's nothing there."

Leaning over my shoulder, Luke tried to make sense of what barely passed as photographs. "Very strange." With a casual shrug of his shoulders, Luke moved on to the bookcases and the slew of books nearly pouring off the shelves.

Even after the incident at Westwood, I still took moments like these with a healthy dose of skepticism—even though it would be easy to read into my camera's behavior.

While exploring an abandoned insane asylum, I had uncovered a decades-old murder and witnessed the suicide of one of my college students at Westwood Asylum for the Insane, which burned to the ground. After that I left my teaching position at the college and spent some time working on my writing and trying to forget.

After that experience, I could no longer say that I did not believe in the paranormal, but I also had to remember that every creak, every drip, every sigh of the building around me, could be construed as some sort of otherworldly occurrence given enough imagination. But I would be lying if I said I hadn't felt the tiniest chill a moment ago.

I tried hard to keep up with Luke not because I thought there was something in the house—quite the opposite—but in case something else happened, something odd. I wanted him there to witness it, so I could talk myself out of whatever supernatural explanation might come to me.

We continued to move quietly through the house until we came to the stairway. This time, as we climbed up to the second floor, I noticed a wooden cabinet above set into the wall at eye level. I reached for the little round knob on the door and pulled, but it did not budge.

I tugged harder and harder until the door let out a massive cracking sound and finally popped open, releasing a waterfall of travel maps that cascaded down the stairs.

"This house just keeps getting weirder and weirder." I shook my head and bent down to sift through the piles of maps. Luke backtracked down the stairs and knelt beside me. "Look at these...California, Washington D.C., Route 66..."

"Greece, Hawaii, England, Japan...I wonder if these people actually went to all these places." He added.

"There must be hundreds of maps in that cabinet." I reached in to see just how far back the cabinet went. "So these people were obviously well read. Multilingual. And apparently world travelers, yet they abandoned their house."

"Curioser and curioser", I whispered then gathered the maps off the stairs and jammed them back into the cabinet. By the time I reached the top of the stairs, Luke had already disappeared...so much for staying close together.

Today I decided to take the time to examine the books in the second-floor bookcase and discovered they were all children's books, both leather-bound classics and hardcover nursery books. A thick green volume with gold-embossed lettering immediately caught my attention, and I slid it out of the crush of books.

"Well I'll be...*Anne of Green Gables*."

I tucked the book under my arm, feeling like it was some sort of sign—though a sign of what, I had no idea—and kept moving. In the guest bedroom behind me, I could hear Luke opening and closing drawers, rummaging through the closet to see what had been left behind.

Joining him in the room, I looked around and noticed how drab and plain this bedroom was compared to the others. There was really nothing appealing in this room, so I turned my camera off and set it down. I started to pick through the items Luke had scattered across the top of the room's double bureau—old political campaign buttons, a checking account register, an empty Chanel No. 5 Eau de Parfum box.

As I set the perfume box back down on the bureau, I heard Luke's voice a few rooms away, rising slightly with a hint of panic. Luke is generally one of the calmest, most laid-back individuals I knew, so for him to show panic of any kind was cause for alarm.

I had a hard time figuring out where he was in the house. The little cottage seemed to have a strange way of distorting sound. Eventually, I found him in the little warren of storage rooms that ran the length of the back wall of the house.

"What is it?" I asked, not realizing at first what was making him panic. He was just standing there, staring into a room wedged in below the steeply pitched roof. Finally it registered what he was looking at inside the room.

There was a light turned on in the room, and there certainly was not one on the first time we were in the house.

"Didn't you come up here last time?" Luke took a step backward and gestured at the room that was filled to the rafters with toys and games.

I nodded. "I went into every room up here and there was no light. I would have noticed a light, especially because that bulb is right at eye level."

Luke was looking around at all the walls, his eyes searching for something he did not seem to be finding. "Where's the switch?"

I, too, began examining every wall and found no switch. "I don't see one." I followed the silver snake of conduit away from the light fixture and down through a hole in the floor. "That's odd. It goes back downstairs. I guess that means the switch is down there?"

Luke frowned. "That's a stupid place for a light switch. And why does this place have power when everything I've found is from the 90's? That's more than a decade ago."

"I don't understand, either. Maybe..." I was digging for an explanation, but my train of thought was derailed by the familiar sound of a camera struggling to focus on an image of something. I listened for a moment, then felt the hair on my arms stand straight up. "Is that my camera trying to focus on something?"

Together Luke and I hurried into the bedroom where I had left my camera set up on the tripod. I expected to see an animal of some kind that would have triggered the auto focus, but there was nothing there. Luke walked right over to my camera and bent down to look at it.

"Abby, I hate to tell you this, but your camera isn't even on."

"But it was focusing. You heard it, too. I'm not crazy, right?"

He nodded. "I definitely heard it, but there's no way it was your camera. It's off."

"What is going on here? This is the second time that my camera has malfunctioned in this house. It's never given me any kind of problem before."

"I think it's time we left," Luke said quietly. "I believe we have overstayed our welcome."

We gathered our camera equipment together and descended the stairs quickly, heading back through the living room toward the kitchen. "Hang on," I said, stopping short in the living room. "I want to check something."

I went over to a green upholstered easy chair that sat next to a combination lamp and telephone table. I twisted the plastic knob on the lamp, and it immediately illuminated the black rotary-dial phone that sat on the table. Quickly, I snapped it back off. Even in broad daylight, I feared someone might notice a light on in the house, as irrational as that thought sounded.

For a second time, I pulled all the doors closed behind us on the way out, hopefully disguising the fact that we had been there—just in case someone truly was watching the house.

Now it was approaching late afternoon and the sun was slung low and bright, just above the peak of the cottage's asphalt roof. A glow seemed to emanate from the glass windowpanes, falling on each petal of each flower, and on the lush green leaves that surrounded Green Gables.

Looking carefully at the quiet house, I suddenly felt that there was something here that simply did not fit, though I had no idea what.

Chapter 2

The house sat silently in the dark, shadows passing over it, flitting through the backyard and into the woods. Fireflies illuminated tiny ovals of sky every few feet, lighting the way for the fluid shapes that floated off towards the lost town of Quabbin. A raccoon waddled out from behind the barn and across the front lawn, stopping in a patch of moonlight that illuminated his little black button eyes. The house was asleep though and the raccoon continued on his way, undisturbed. The single occupant of the house, however, was awake and alert.

***

Blackbird Road looked distinctly different on Google Maps. The hybrid aerial photos of the neighborhood that surrounded Green Gables were far less developed, apparently having been taken some time before the area had grown into the little enclave that it was now.

Not knowing the number of the house, it took more time than before to locate the cottage amongst the trees. Suddenly there it was, set back from the road, isolated from its neighbors. I took a screen shot of the satellite map and attached it to an e-mail that I fired off to a woman named Mary Ellen, who worked for the Registrar of Deeds for the State of Massachusetts. I asked her to send any information she could find about the cottage.

After sending the email, I sat back and pulled out the battered yet remarkably intact copy of *Anne of Green Gables* that I had brought home with me. It was a beautiful pine-green color with a simple, lively title font and a flower embossed on the cover. The volume had been printed in 1959 and was in wonderful shape, a simply beautiful book.

I began flipping through the pages, admiring the illustrations. As I continued to leaf through it, a small piece of paper fell out of the book and onto the floor. I picked it up and found that it was a photograph of a young girl standing in front of the cottage wearing a white dress.

The photo certainly predated the book by a number of years. In fact, if I was to hazard a guess, the photograph was from the mid-to-late 1800s. Unfortunately, there was nothing written on the back of the picture—no name, no date—but it was the first concrete piece of the house's history that I could hold.

***

A few days after visiting the cottage, a large manila envelope arrived in the mail postmarked from Grafton. Mary Ellen had come through after all. I opened the envelope to find a thick pile of papers and a handwritten letter explaining the documents.

Abby:

I pulled the deeds on the property as far back as 1800. There have only been a couple of owners, so it was fairly easy

to find. The property was a small farm owned by the Murray family
until the late 1980s when the last surviving relative passed and
the house was put up for auction. It was converted into some sort of
rooming house and was occupied until 1991 when the bank foreclosed
due to non-payment of the mortgage. After that, however, the house became
property of a land trust, assuming it held some sort of historical
significance. The land and the house can no longer be sold or occupied,
nor can it be demolished, but there was no further information as to
why. You might want to check the town records. Hope this helps!

Mary Ellen

The rest of the documents were photocopies of type-written deeds documenting property lines and rightful owners. It was easy to follow the Murray family as the farm passed from one generation to the next, then to a stranger, and finally to the mysterious land trust.

I opened up the Internet browser on my laptop and typed the address of the cottage. Very little came up aside from obituaries for members of the Murray family and brief records of the deed transfers. The one interesting piece of information was a reference to the Civil War and the town's role in abolition. That was certainly something worth digging into. I decided to head to the town hall in spite of the long drive.

The offices were fairly deserted. I showed my packet of papers from Mary Ellen to the woman behind the counter and asked if any other information was available. Pushing her zebra print readers onto the bridge of her nose, the fussy-looking middle-aged woman skimmed the papers and sighed quickly.

"Well, it might take a bit of digging, but let me try."

She returned with a painfully small pile of papers and slapped them onto the copy machine behind her.

"That'll be $3.35 for the copies. Here." She tossed them across the counter at me.

I debated thanking her, but she had already turned her back to me, pretending to be busy with something more important. I headed outside to my car and shuffled quickly through the papers. The first story to catch my eye was a handwritten report from a townsperson who had documented a fire behind the Murray cottage. I read through it, my jaw slack with surprise.

A fire had started in the woods behind the house, supposedly set by townspeople sympathetic to the rebel cause, in order to send a message to the Murrays, who were suspected of aiding slaves in escaping to the towns of Dana, Enfield, and Greenwich. It immediately struck me that the Quabbin Reservoir did not yet exist at the time of the Civil War. The story went on to say that no one was hurt, and no slaves were discovered, but the rebel sympathizers were convinced that the Murray farm had hidden underground tunnels leading beneath the tree line.

Could that house have tunnels underneath? I thought back to the expansive backyard, the thick forest that formed its boundaries. We had not gone down into the basement, so I could not say for certain if it was possible to hide a tunnel entrance somewhere.

I called Luke and left a fairly lengthy voicemail message explaining everything I had learned. Other than the first-person report describing the fire, there was not much of interest, although I found myself flipping through all the pages again. Then I picked up the phone and called Luke again, intending to leave him another message, but this time he answered the phone.

"Hey, I just listened to your message. That's pretty dope that there might be tunnels."

I shuffled the pile of papers while we talked. "I know how this is going to sound, but maybe that explains the weird camera stuff. A connection to the Underground Railroad could point to quite a history behind the cottage. I can't imagine—if all that is true— just how many people passed through that house."

"Do you want to try to go back?"

"Yeah...I'd like to see if there are actually tunnels. It'd be really cool to see if maybe there's anything left down there."

"You're fine with the weirdness in the house?"

I shrugged to myself. "I don't see a problem with it. If there truly is something in that house, I'm sure we'll know for certain pretty quickly."

"Ok, then. Saturday again?"

"Sounds good."

And so, on Saturday morning, we once again pulled onto the lawn and crossed over the barbed wire fences that once served to keep deer out of the gardens. The window at the back of the house was still open and the cooler was still in the same place, but I wanted to take a quick look around the backyard first, just to see if there was evidence of tunnels visible from above ground.

The grass, a beautiful rich green carpet, had been cut recently and smelled fresh and crisp. Flowering bushes formed a natural fence line on one side of the yard leading toward the edge of the woods, though I couldn't for the life of me identify the blooms. Wandering over to the bushes, I stopped to smell the magenta-colored blossoms. I stepped closer and my toe hit something hard.

Looking down, I realized that I had kicked a pile of concrete and rock that was half- hidden by grass and moss. "Luke, come over here."

Joining me in the backyard, Luke looked down as well. "Wow. Are you thinking that might be the top of a tunnel?"

I shrugged. "I suppose it's a possibility."

***

Inside the house, the air was stale and humid. The moisture intensified the odor of mold and age, but everything appeared to be exactly as we left it the last time.

Luke's eyes darted around as we crossed into the living room. "Let's check out the basement first."

We headed through the living room to where there was a door we assumed led to the basement. But on impulse, I veered instead toward the easy chair and reached out to turn on the lamp on the telephone table. This time the clicking switch produced nothing but a short echo of sound.

"The power's been cut."

"Maybe the power company finally had enough." Luke was laughing, but I could tell he, too, found it strange that after all these years the power would suddenly be turned off.

With flashlights illuminating small yellow puddles at our feet, we descended into the basement and a damp chill. We were greeted by a dirt cellar with fieldstone walls that had obviously been cut right into the ground. The room itself was wholly unremarkable—nothing but a large, low ceilinged square under the original house.

It appeared that the only access to the basement was the staircase we had just used. We had to duck in order to move around the room, brushing spider webs from our hair and faces. Strangely the basement seemed to be the only room that was completely empty which we both found rather odd. As we ventured deeper into the room my flashlight caught the outline of barn doors on one of the far walls but it looked to me like they simply opened onto the side yard near the big red barn near the street.

"I don't see anything Abby. These walls are solid rock."

Looking around I had to agree. There was no sign of a tunnel anywhere. I walked closer to one of the walls and put my hand out, touching the field stones, the surface of which were cold and damp, yet soft with a fine coating of moss. Luke was right, the walls were solid and there was no sign of a break in the wall or a hidden access point. "Maybe the tunnel thing is just hearsay," I conceded, disappointed, but I kept my hand to the walls as I circled the basement. "Why do you suppose there's plywood over this part of the wall?" I hadn't noticed it before but someone had managed to attach a four foot by eight foot piece of plywood to a part of the foundation wall. "What do you think?"

Luke tried to stick his hand behind the plywood but there wasn't a whole lot of space behind it. "It looks like it's lag bolted to the stone."

"Damn. I guess that means we're not taking it off."

"You know, why don't we go check out the barn and see if there's a saw or a crowbar or something."

It wasn't a bad idea. "Luke, that's brilliant. This is why I keep you around."

He shook his head at me and chuckled, then headed for the stairs to go up. We had to follow the maze through the bedrooms to the back of the house, into the sunroom that connected to the barn.

"That's encouraging." I reached out and grabbed the police tape across the door. "Let's see if we can do this without breaking our necks."

Even right on the other side of the door the considerable damage in the barn was evident. The floor had collapsed, cabinets, shelves, and work tables pitched at dangerous angles looking as if the smallest breeze might trigger a massive slide into the vortex in the middle of the room.

"Hey Luke...the barn has a lower level too."

We both stared down into the gaping hole at the dirt floor below us. Luke pointed to the far edge of the collapse. "There's a ladder stuck in some of the debris."

"Yeah but you would have to climb across the edge of the collapse to get to it."

"So?" Sometimes Luke's willingness to take a risk astounded me. I remember once watching him climb an eight foot anti-climb fence only to roll over three strips of barbed wire and drop down into two feet of snow on the other side, all while security made rounds. Needless to say I chickened out that day and found another, easier way in. Luke dropped to his knees and started to crawl and pull himself toward the ladder. Every time he reached out to grab the shelving anchored to the wall, I watched it pull away from its mooring just a little bit more. I held my breath, my heart stopping with each crack of the jagged floorboards that lined the edge of the collapse, as they were the only things standing between Luke and a messy plunge into the darkness below. Finally after what seemed like hours, but was likely only minutes, Luke made it to the ladder and began to descend to the lower level. There was no way in hell I was following him unless there was something good down there so I stood in the doorway and listened to him shuffling around below me.

"Abby, you need to get down here," Luke yelled up to me.

"Oh dear God. I'm going to end up killing myself." I yelled. Or at the very least, breaking a few very important appendages, but still I knelt and began to crawl across the floor the same way Luke did, again watching the shelving shake as if there was an earthquake sweeping through the barn. I realized I was holding my breath again and didn't let it out until I was able to stretch my foot out and put it firmly on the top rung of the ladder which was almost as shaky as the floor itself. Thankfully I looked down to see Luke standing below me, ready to save me should I totally bite it off the ladder.

Once I was on firm ground I waited a moment for my eyes to adjust to the darkness, then looked around until I saw what had Luke so excited. On the far side of the barn, facing the backyard, was a wooden door. A wooden door with a heavy black padlock. We stood and considered the door, wondering whether or not we should attempt to open it. Curiosity certainly was running strong but suddenly we were distracted by a low rumbling coming from above us, kicking up a cloud of dust, followed by chunks of debris.

"What's happening?" I cried. "What's going on?"

Luke looked up just in time to see the shelves from the workshop pull completely away from the wall and come crashing through to the basement, taking the ladder with it. A chain reaction followed as tools, tables, drawers, and chairs rained down through the chasm. Then the giant work bench that had been anchored to the wall across from the shelves let out a shriek and a groan as it too pulled away, taking a large portion of the wall and floor with it. It happened so quickly that it took a moment for us to realize that the barn was collapsing in on us and the only way out was the wooden door that was locked tight.

"Luke we need to get out of here!" He could barely hear me over the roar of wood and metal collapsing into the space.

He turned, looking around for another escape route but I already knew he wouldn't find one, but then it looked as if an idea had suddenly dawned on him and he picked up a chunk of wooden beam that had landed on the floor, ramming it against the door over and over. IT was hard to tell if it was doing any good since we couldn't hear over the din of destruction but the next blow split the door in the middle and Luke commenced kicking and beating the door until there was a space big enough to scramble through. Without a second thought we dived through the hole and into the darkness behind it. We crawled as far and as fast as we could until we could no longer hear the barn imploding. The moment we stopped I rolled onto my back and tried to catch my breath. Luke collapsed beside me and we sat in silence, trying to wrap our heads around what had just happened.

"Abby, are you okay?"

"I think so. You?"

I could feel him nodding in the darkness. "I can't believe that whole floor just collapsed. We were damned lucky we got through that door."

"Where are we though? I think I lost my flashlight at some point."

Luke rustled around a bit and then suddenly we were bathed in light. We were surrounded by packed brick walls, a dirt floor, and a low brick ceiling. Turning the flashlight ahead we could only see a few feet in front of us, the darkness beyond seemed endless.

"Abby. We're in a tunnel."

Chapter 3

I know very little about Civil War history as it's absolutely not my forte but I did know for certain that we were in a slave tunnel. Unfortunately the excitement of finding of finding ourselves in the tunnel gave way to the fear that we might possibly be trapped. Retracing our steps to the beginning of the tunnel, we could see through the hole in the door that it was completely blocked by debris. Our only choice was to move forward not knowing how long the tunnel actually was, or for that matter, whether or not there would be another way out if we even managed to find the end.

"So I'm completely terrified but at the same time totally fascinated," I laughed, looking around at the thick brick walls. "But man this could go bad fast."

"Yes it could," Luke agreed. "I think the smartest thing we can do is move and see if we can find the spot in the backyard that collapsed. We might have a shot at pushing our way out."

We started out and carefully picked our way across the dirt floor, watching where we put our feet not just because we were being careful but also because we hoped that there might be something tangible left behind in the tunnel.

"Oh I almost forgot to tell you. I took a copy of 'Anne of Green Gables' from the shelves upstairs and when I opened it there was a photo of a little girl stuck inside."

"Really? Was she a Murray?"

I shook my head. "Not sure. The photo wasn't labeled. No name, no date."

"Interesting. Too bad there's no information."

We continued walking, Luke sweeping his flashlight over every surface, making sure we hadn't missed a possible exit, but so far the tunnel was tight as a drum. It had been built well, the bricks cleanly mortared, the dirt floor packed flat beneath our feet. Halfway down the tunnel was a wooden chair pushed against the left wall but it looked rather more modern than the tunnel itself, which suggested that there was access to the tunnel for many years after the end of the Civil War. Unfortunately there wasn't much else, but we were growing more concerned with finding a way out than with sightseeing. Finally after walking quite a bit farther we could see signs of grass and dirt piled on the floor of the tunnel. There was no light shining down but still the dirt was a good sign. That meant the ceiling was weak.

Another great bit of luck dawned when we noticed another chair sitting in the middle of the tunnel. I went over and bent to grab the chair and as I did, noticed a white lump underneath it. I stretched to reach it and realized my fingers had connected with cloth of some kind. Once I had it in my hand I turned it over to find that I was holding a doll. I grabbed both it and the chair, dragging the chair over to the spot we hoped would allow us to escape. Luke positioned the chair in the middle of the tunnel and climbed up on it, but still he needed to stretch a bit in order to touch the top. He pushed on a couple different spots, and then pushed harder and harder until a shower of dirt and grass came raining down on him. I couldn't help but laugh, doubling over and slapping my knees as he spit dirt out of his mouth and wiped it from him eyes.

"Laugh all you want," he said. "I'm the one who's going to have to boost you up through this hole. You keep making fun of me I'll leave you down here!"

"It worked?"

Luke moved and I could see a small halo of light poking through the ceiling of the tunnel. "I have to make it bigger but yeah it worked." He kept digging until he was able to grab eth edge of the hole and pull himself up to his shoulders, his head disappearing aboveground. "Ok I'll boost you up first then I'll pull myself out behind you."

I tucked the doll under my arm and traded places with him on the chair. Luke laced his fingers together in front of his chest and waiting for me to put my foot in his hands. Without warning he rocketed me up and through the hole. In one graceless move I dropped the door on the ground and belly flopped on top of its stiff little body."

With the wind knocked out of me, I rolled away from the opening and lay on my back, struggling to catch my breath. Luke came vaulting out a moment later, far more fluidly than I had with nothing more than a minute expulsion of breath.

I stood and brushed off my pants to no avail. The grass stains were now permanent from the look of it. With my hand I shielded my eyes from the sun and looked off into the woods where the sun had begun to set. "Can you imagine how far that tunnel must go?"

Luke was busy trying to hide the hole in the ground that we had created, packing dirt, grass, and chunks of rock back on the pile. By the time he was finished he had actually done a fairly good job of covering our tracks. He stood, stretched his back, and brushed the remains of his digging from this palms. "My guess is it went all the way out to the Quabbin, though the reservoir would have been nonexistent at the time."

"The towns would still have been there and there would have been people living there. I wonder if there was an entire network of tunnels in this area. That wouldn't have been uncommon."

Luke shrugged. "I doubt there's any way to find out for certain."

"I've heard of a number of New England homes," I said, "that have recorded the existence of tunnels or hiding places from the Civil War. But the documentation is still pretty sparse."

I bent to pick up the doll and tucked it under my arm, then headed back to the window. "We need to go get our gear and get out of here. I feel like I got run over."

"I'll get it. Why don't you wait out here." Luke patted my arm and hoisted himself into the open window to retrieve our bags from inside the house.

So chivalry wasn't dead after all. I headed back out into the yard and sat down in the sun with the doll in my lap. It was a small, chubby thing with a soft body and a china head. Somehow she had survived with little more than a chip on the tip of her nose and some mighty snarls in her blond, stringy hair. Her white dress was dirty and yellowed, her little black shoes scuffed and faded. My first thought was perhaps she belonged to the little girl in the photograph I had found in the book. My second thought was, what was she doing down in the tunnel?

In my mind there seemed to be no reason for a child to be that deep in a tunnel, especially as I imagined it was just as dark down there back then as well. Of course it piqued my curiosity, wondering if there was some mystery of sorts behind the doll in the tunnel, but then perhaps letting myself consider that idea wasn't the best.

Behind me I could hear Luke climbing through the window on his way back out. He lowered the bags to the ground and then lowered himself as well. He grabbed a bag in each hand and came over to join me.

"Well, that certainly was interesting." Luke tucked his bag behind his head and leaned back, closing his eyes.

"I suppose it depends on how you define interesting."

Luke chuckled, his arms crossed over his chest bouncing up and down as he laughed. "We found something very, very cool but I don't think I ever want to be almost crushed by a building ever again."

"Agreed. Though this is technically the second time we've narrowly escaped a building that was self destructing."

"True, but the way I see it, a slow burning monolith isn't nearly as terrifying as having pieces of a barn coming straight at your head."

Now it was my turn to laugh. "You have a point my friend."

Luke rolled on his side and reached out toward one of the bushes nearest us and came back with a handful of blackberries, handing me a few. We chewed in silence as the sun ducked slowly behind the trees, a glow spreading across the year. Dusk had descended quickly and it completely changed the look of the cottage. Now it seemed to crouch in the waning sunlight rather than stretching to meet the bright morning rays. Shadows also began to materialize at the edges of the yard and around the trunks of the trees. We stood and headed back to the car, swinging our tired legs over the barbed wire. Slinging our bags into the car I suddenly had the feeling that someone was watching me. I turned to look back at the house, scanning each window, and I could have sworn I saw the curtains swing back into place in one of the second floor windows.

"He Luke." I pointed up to the second floor. "What room is that right there?"

"Not sure. I think it's that tiny room in the corner. The kid's room."

I shook my head to clear it, then looked up again but the curtains were still. My imagination was getting away from me. I shook my head once more, climbed into the car with Luke, and headed home.

***

That evening I sat with a cup of tea, the heat on, holding the doll in my lap, replaying the day in my head. We were lucky our curiosity hadn't killed us. *Again.* Yet I couldn't help thinking about the little girl in the photo. I stood and crossed into my office, taking "Anne of Green Gables" off the shelf and flipping it open to the photo. I turned it over and over in my hands, inspecting every inch but still there was no way of knowing who she was. However, as I looked at it once again something in the corner of the scene caught my eye-- laying on the floor behind the girl was the little blond doll, though she looked far cleaner and in better repair than the tiny body laying on my couch. So it *had* belonged to the little girl. I took the photo back to the living room with me and sat back down, pulling the doll to me as if touching her might somehow connect me to the little girl and perhaps tell me who she was, and why her doll was abandoned in that tunnel.

I looked again at the cleaner incarnation of the doll in the photo and noticed that even then, in her neatest state, she had a darker mark at the hem of her dress. I picked up the doll and tried to locate the spot, which turned out to be embroidery. Though crusted over with dirt, it looked to me as if the thread was once a light shade of blue, but it was far too filthy to tell what it actually was. I carried her into the kitchen and stripped off her little dress, running hot water in the stainless steel sink. I carefully placed the doll on the counter and began to run the dress under the water, rubbing the cloth together until the dirt had washed away down the drain. The embroidery had also come clean and it appeared to be a monogram, an elegant cursive curl of letters: *B.M.* Did the "M" perhaps stand for Murray?

I hung the miniature dress on the drying rack next to the load of laundry I had done he day before, then set to dry in front of the space heater mounted in the kitchen wall. I headed for my room and threw on knee socks and my flannel pajamas, beginning to feel the excitement of the day dragging through my muscles, sapping the last of my energy. Falling into bed with my car, I was asleep almost immediately, apparently so tired that I slept through the night without a single dream.

Chapter 4

Jim Hollings climbed on his aging riding mower, tucked a bottle of Miller Lite between his knees, and took off to mow his lawn. It only took him about a half an hour to finish his own yard but he also had to truck all the way down the street to mow the Murray farm, so he started early in order to beat the heat. Even though it was only 10:00 am he justified his early morning alcohol consumption by reminding himself that it would take him almost 11:00 to finish the first one and by the time he went back in the house, grabbed his second beer, and climbed back on his mower to head to the Murray's it would be almost noon which was a perfectly acceptable hour for drinking.

Humming tunelessly Hollings made short work of his yard. He loved taking a whole Sunday to mow because by the time he got back in the house and showered his wife would have dinner ready and she'd rub his shoulders while he ate in front of the TV. With a second beer held tight in his hand Jim pulled his mower onto the street and rumbled toward the farm, pulling onto the front lawn where he dropped the mower deck and resumed humming. He never even noticed the face peering down at him from the second floor.

He did however notice the plywood hanging loose off the window in the back. "God damned nosy kids," he muttered, shaking his head in disgust. It had been a while since he had seen signs of intruders but it had certainly been an issue over the past few years since he had taken over the maintenance of the Murray place from the old guy, Mr. Osbourne. Osbourne had had a heart attack while mowing this very yard with his ancient push mower. Just dropped dead right there. The neighbors who had been around when it happened said the mower just sat in one place and ran until it was completely out of gas. That's how they knew something was wrong. The old guy's wife heard the mower stop and she waited almost an hour for him to come home but he didn't. She sent her grandson to get the old man so the kid was the one who found him. He ran back to his grandmother, crying and screaming that his grandpa was dead. The rest of the neighbors heard the commotion and came out to see what was going on. That kid had a hell of a set of lungs seeing as most of the houses were almost a mile apart. Later the neighbors would say his eyes were wide open like he had been scared to death.

Getting off his mower Hollings headed around the front of the house to get something to fix the window with. He headed to the barn and unlocked the padlock. He wrestled with the sliding door a minute, kicking and cursing at it until it ground open.

"What in the hell happened in here?" Hollings peered down into the wreckage of the barn. "The damned thing collapsed!"

Hollings slammed the barn door angrily and turned on his heel, intending to go home and call the police. He headed back to his mower, his head down, still grumbling, oblivious to the fact that his mower was on fire.

Chapter 5

A week later Luke and I again decided to pay a visit to Green Gables. My intention was to go through every book, ever corner, and every pile of paper in the house, hoping to find out who the little girl in the photo was. We went to pull onto the lawn in the same place but were stopped by new strings of barbed wire, so we were forced to park in a layby farther down Blackbird Road and walk back to the house It was nerve racking to be walking out in the open like that but like both other times we had visited, the road was all but deserted. Entering from this new angle I immediately fell in love with the charm of the cottage that stood at the end of a winding leafy path that lead to the front door. It was like something out of a storybook.

Coming around to the back of the house we found the wild rose bushes at the edge of the property beginning to bud. The gardens on the property must have been beautiful at one time when someone was still caring for them. I imagined the generations of Murray women tending the curtains of flowers that surrounded the cottage.

"Obviously someone truly is watching this place but why the new barbed wire?" Had someone seen us go in and reported us?

Luke lifted his foot and brought his work boot down on the barbed wire, stretching it to the ground so I could step over safely. The moment we crossed into the backyard we knew something wasn't right but we didn't realize what it was until we looked down and noticed the enormous scorch marks in the middle of the yard.

"What the hell happened here?" Luke bent and placed his hand on the blackened grass. "That explains the new barbed wire. Something must have happened. Within the last few days from the look of it."

I looked up at the back of the house to see that someone had also replaced the plywood on the window and removed the red cooler. There was also a 'No Trespassing' sign hung on a strip of barbed wire strung on metal poles between two blackberry bushes nearest the house.

"It must have been something rather serious. They sealed up our window too."

Luke looked up at the cottage as well. "Do you want to skip it then?"

I shook my head. "No. I can't say I'm particularly worried. Most likely a bunch of kids had some sort of party out here and were stupid enough to have a fire. Let's just make sure we close everything up behind us so it's not obvious we were here. We should be fine."

I skirted the barbed wire and approached the window, pulling a screwdriver out of my bag. Though the red cooler had been taken I was able to find a few loose bricks to stand on so I could reach the top of the window frame. I removed all but one screw so that we could swing the plywood out of the way, then let it fall back into place.

I again struggled through the window and into the pantry, Luke close behind me. Though once inside the house things seemed different inside as well; darker perhaps. I crossed into the living room only to find that someone had drawn all the shades, hence the darkness. That meant I would have to pull out my flashlight in order to dig through everything. Since the living room windows faced the road it would be far too risky to raise the shades. Flashlight in hand I began reading each book title though may of them were not in English. I pulled a few random volumes off the shelves and thumbed through them but none seemed to hold anything more than mold and moisture. However, the bottom shelf looked as if it held a few books that might have had papers stuffed inside them.

Lowering myself to the floor I pulled a few books off the shelf, removing the papers from them and putting them aside. After working for a bit I had a fairly sizable pile of papers, which I slid into my bag to sift through later. I carefully replaced the books and moved on to the bedrooms where I found little more than Band-Aids, mouth wash, and a little plastic alarm clock. I then crossed through the bathroom (empty but for a hand towel) and found myself in an almost pitch black bedroom with piles of junk in every corner. Unfortunately upon inspection it was all modern items, most likely left behind by the most recent boarders. The next room was the strange junk room that connected the original house to the addition, the only room that had been boarded up completely. I picked through boxes of books, piles of record albums crawling with silverfish, and collections of notebooks but again nothing truly belonged to the house, only to the boarders. I sighed as I stood and retraced my steps, heading for the main stairs to the second floor.

I performed the same search on the top floor as well finding nothing promising in any of the bedrooms. I also searched the collection of children's books again, this time more thoroughly, but found nothing more of the little girl. Finally I headed for the tiny room under the eaves. The walls were painted a dark green, peeling in some spots to reveal patches of light yellow underneath. The bed was certainly a child's, smaller than a modern day twin bed, with a stained blue and white striped mattress and dingy white pillow. I bent to put my hand on the mattress only to find, to my great surprise, that it was actually stuffed with hay and grass, the pillow with feathers. At the foot of the bed a small lamp perched on an equally tiny end table at the foot of the bed. A chair, painted green to match the walls, was pushed into the corner near the only window in the room. It was a cozy little space, perfect for a child; that is if it had been clean and bright as it was meant to be.

Other than the furniture the room was empty, but just on a whim I dropped to the floor and looked under the bed. My flashlight beam just barely illuminated the space under the bed, the light having been reduced to a sickly yellow glow. I sat back on my heels and shook the flashlight, slapping it against my palm but still the light remained dim. I crouched back down to take another look under the bed but still the back corners were not illuminated. In the next moment I heard a faint click from above and suddenly everything was bathed in light, including the small box wedged in the corner farthest from me. Dropping to my stomach I stretched my arm under the tiny bed and grabbed the box, dragging it toward me. I sat up with it on my lap and stared in wonder at the little lamp, twinkling away on the table. Struggling to my feet I took off running, yelling for Luke.

He met me on the stairs, drawn by my high volume hysterics. "Abby, what are you screaming about?"

"The light is on. In the kid's room. It just clicked on."

Luke grabbed me by the shoulders and shook me. "The power is off Abby. You checked, remember?"

"I swear. It's on. I'm not crazy."

I grabbed his hand and dragged him towards the room, the box still tucked under my arm, but when we got to the door the room within was dark. "No! This isn't possible!" I ran from room to room throwing switches and flicking on laps, my frustration growing along with the darkness. Luke trailed behind me, trying in vain to get me to calm down, but I couldn't stop. I didn't stop until we came around to the storage room where Luke had first discovered that there was power in the house. There, in that storage room, the light was on.

"See! This one's on!"

Luke screeched to a stop, almost like a cartoon character stopping short before getting brained by a safe or a piano. Every piece of childhood stacked in that room was brilliantly illuminated, all of it piled haphazardly along each wall. It looked like generations of board games, baseball gloves, and stuffed animals. There were no windows anywhere around us so it was quite a shock when a crack of thunder split the silence in the house like a firecracker-- and the lights went out.

Chapter 6

Out in the woods the thunder rolled through the tree branches, shaking them to their roots. With every thunder strike, a flash of lightning followed moments later, illuminating a face amongst the trees. He had gotten out of the house by the skin of his teeth when those two came back. He knew it wasn't smart to keep returning to the house but the house called to him and drew him in day after day.

In the light of the next flash he looked at his watch, then at the sky. The rain was fast on its way and he needed to get home before his wife realized he had left the house again. He turned and headed back through the woods, following the path he had used to get here that led back into his own yard.

Inside the house he could see his wife bustling around the kitchen, no doubt getting dinner ready. Probably some dry tasteless roast of something. He loved her dearly but her cooking was atrocious. She mercifully did not look up and so he managed to sneak by and in the front door, then into the kitchen where he pretended he had just come in from the garage. Kissing his wife on the cheek, he backtracked to the living room and settled in to read the paper.

Chapter 7

We resisted the urge to run. The thunder continued to roll and we continued to count the seconds between rumbles and flashes of light. The storm was going to be an impressive one, the wind howling around the house, lashing at the shutters and the loose roof tiles. By the time we had hurried down the stairs and into the living room the rain had begun to fall, first in heavy, sloppy drops. Then it began to drive harder, hitting the windowpanes sideways at such a force that the shades on the inside of the window quivered. In the kitchen the torrents of rain actually poured in through the broken window, soaking the top of the kitchen table and forming tiny rivers that ran across and onto the floor. The wind too picked up in intensity, making a whistling noise through the jagged holes in the glass. It created a tiny wind tunnel that caught hold of the living room door and slammed it shut.

"I have a feeling we would be better off waiting in here until the storm dies down," Luke said, retreating into the center of the living room, away from the windows.

I did the same, dropping down onto the large couch that had been arranged in front of the fireplace, well away from each bank of windows. Though the temperature outside was still a muggy ninety plus degrees, a chill passed through the inside of the house, carried by the winds of the storm and the damp of the rain. I hadn't thought to bring a sweatshirt and was now regretting not being able to cover up as a shiver ran down my spine. "Hopefully it will pass quickly, though it might have rolled over the reservoir first which would make it pick up force rather than slow down."

Luke shook his head as he leaned against the fireplace. "You have the most eclectic mass of knowledge in that head of yours don't you."

"Yes I suppose I do," I laughed, crossing my arms over my chest in an attempt to stave off another chill. I sat and stared at the windows though the shades were still drawn so there was nothing to see but the subtle swaying of the dirty yellow material as it floated on the draft coming through the window frames. The rain and wind raged outside, buffeting the little cottage as it was trying to teach it a lesson for being in the path of nature on a rampage, but the house took it well, swaying and creaking only a bit, showing its age only occasionally. Unfortunately the air of relative safety was only an illusion. As I continued to stare a gust of wind pounded the back side of the house and the bay windows that looked in on the bookcases to our left popped, then shattered, the shades whipping up and rolling themselves around and around. The rain followed the glass, mixing with the shards to create dangerous puddles on the floor.

I realized I had screamed and instinctively covered my head. Luke had dropped to the floor, also shielding his eyes from the sudden intrusion of weather. The roar that enveloped the living room was overwhelming and we had to shout to be heard above the din.

"We need to get down to the basement," Luke bellowed. "I think this storm just turned into a hurricane!"

We grabbed our bags and Luke wrenched open the door to the basement but at the threshold I hesitated. "Hang on! I'll be right back!" I pitched my camera bag in his direction and dodged around the corner into the bedroom where I stripped both beds of their coverlets, blankets, sheets, and pillows. I struggled to gather everything up as another blast of wind shattered the windows right in front of me, blowing glass and leaves all over the room. I ducked, pillows and blankets wrapped around my arms, and crab walked to the basement door. I tumbled down the first couple of stairs and, after I regained my balance, I reached back up to yank the door shut behind me. Luke was at the bottom of the stairs, waiting to grab some of the blankets from me, then led me to a corner that he seemed to have decided was safest. We spread the two sheets on the floor and wrapped ourselves in the blankets, then threw the coverlets over us in a makeshift fort. That way we were both protected with our camera bags next to us.

"I guess one of us should have checked the weather this morning," I joked, laughing nervously. Storms didn't necessarily make me nervous but I certainly wasn't excited by the thought of yet another portion of this house collapsing on us.

Luke and I sat back on the pillows and listened to the storm swirling around us, the house creaking and moaning as the wind whipped through the now completely broken windows upstairs. At some point we both must have dozed off because it seemed like only moments later that the storm had subsided but when I looked at the display on my cell phone it had been three hours and my phone's battery was almost dead.

Thought it seemed to have quieted down outside we still continued to wait just to be sure before collecting our bags and slowly climbing back to the surface. There was carnage everywhere in the house-- glass, mud, puddles of water, bits of grass-- covering the carpet in the living room and the bedroom I had stripped of its bedding. It seemed that it was only the windows at the back that had broken but the damage was considerable. Furniture had toppled over and lay scattered amidst tattered strips of shades and soaking wet books that had fallen from the shelves.

There was no discussion-- we needed to get out of that house as quickly as possible. Without wasting a second more we were out the window, over the barbed wire, and at the car in record time. Though in a hurry I still paused to look up at the house and this time I definitely saw a hand part the curtains of the child's bedroom.

"Oh my God. The box!" I had forgotten the box I had pulled out from under the bed. "Luke, I have to go back in!" I tossed my bag into the car and took off around the house, the thorns tearing into my arms as I ran, stumbling over the deer fences and slipping on the wet grass. I tried my best to get in the window but wound up hitting my head on the wooden frame so hard I was sure I was about to faint. I burst into the living room where the box was still sitting on the couch where I had been moments before the windows exploded. Bending to pick up the box I felt a remarkably cold breeze sweep down my spine, so I instinctively looked up and there she was, just for a moment, the girl in the photograph was standing right in front of me.

And then, in the blink of an eye, she was gone.

Chapter 8

The moment I got home I climbed into a hot shower and tried to wash away the chill that had settled into my bones. Between the storm and the apparition my mind was full to bursting. Full of questions, full of shock-- yet not full of surprise. The incident at Westwood had started with a photo, so why shouldn't it happen again? I climbed out of the shower and wrapped myself in a towel, still shivering in spite of the summer heat. I threw on sweatpants and my favorite Pioneer College t-shirt, then tied my wet hair into a bun. I looked in the mirror at the bags under my eyes that had been there since Westwood, my usually bright blue eyes taking on a gray hue that was almost as washed out as my skin tone. I looked terrible.

Sighing, I turned off the bathroom light and headed into the kitchen to start the teakettle. All of the windows in the apartment were open and the temperature had finally settled into something resembling comfort. I leaned on the stove and closed my eyes, listening to the water starting to rattle in the glass kettle. Sometimes I wondered if living alone was beginning to take its toll on my mind. I was finding myself spending far too much time inside my own head, but I also knew myself well enough to be certain I could never stand living with someone else. When I first moved into my apartment I had a steady boyfriend who came and went on a regular basis but I always felt an odd sense of relief when he left and I had the house to myself again. I had considered taking in a roommate but only briefly as I realized I was far too particular to allow someone in my space who may not have the same habits or be as neat or as quiet. Quiet being the most important.

So I continued to live on my own with my precise level of organization and strictly defined spaces and I continued to wonder if that needed to change to change as I carried my tea into my office and sat down in front of my typewriter. I sat and stared at the blank sheet of onionskin sticking out of the platen, drawing a complete blank. A little meow and the pressure of paws on my thigh brought me out of my momentary stupor and Riley hopped into my lap. As he settled in and began to purr, I found myself placing my fingers on the keys and beginning to write. I wrote for two straight hours, the cat out cold, stretched out on my knees. I looked at the stack of sheets on my desk and realized I had written twenty-three pages about Westwood.

***

The sun returned by morning, drying things out after the storm the day before. It was Sunday and the town of Pioneer was quiet as it always was the day before the new work week. I sat out on my deck with my feet up on the rail and a mug of tea in my hand looking out at the horizon where I could see wispy marshmallow clouds hanging over Stone Point in the distance. The day had dawned so beautifully clear that it almost seemed the storm had never happened but the morning news had reported severe storm damage and power outages across the state. The other evidence that yesterday hadn't been a product of my overactive imagination was the little locked box sitting on my coffee table.

Yes it was locked, and no I hadn't yet tried to open it because I wasn't sure I wanted to see what was inside. When I got involved with Westwood Asylum every item I found brought me deeper and deeper into the mystery surrounding the death of one of the asylum's patients. In that same vein I had now found a photograph inside a book, found a locked box, and seen the spirit of a little girl. It seemed as if history was attempting to repeat itself. Did I really want to get involved in whatever was residing in that house? Most like not, but I assume I had already unlatched Pandora's Box and was fast on my way to opening it as I knew my curiosity would eventually win out. Today however I planned to get away from all things paranormal and take the cat on a visit to my parents' house.

My second cup of tea that day was consumed at my mother's kitchen table while the cat sunned himself in the back hall. She had the door open and he was catching the rays that slanted in from the backyard. My mother always said she would never be able to move from that house because she would never be able to recreate that backyard. At the height of summer she managed to concoct a sort of manicured wilderness of purple irises, dahlias, roses, and all manner of flowering trees and bushes that looked very much like a spread in *Better Homes and Gardens.*

"So, I assume you heard about that terrible fire up at Westwood Asylum?"

My mother may have known about my penchant for abandoned buildings but she was still in the dark as to my involvement in Cameron Voegel's death and the raging inferno at the hospital. She was bustling around the kitchen as she talked, starting another round of tea and fishing in the pantry for a snack of sorts.

"Yeah I heard." I tried to be as noncommittal as possible, praying the emotion that immediately rose at the mention of the incident didn't surface in my voice. There was no reason to alarm my mother. "Hey do you think I could have some irises for my yard?" I asked, changing the subject rather abruptly.

My mother looked up and blinked as if I had slapped her, but recovered nicely from my sudden desire to avoid the topic. "Sure. Do you want some of your grandmother's irises, or do you want the ones you dug up at Belchertown State School last summer?"

Thankfully she was all for aiding and abetting my collection of mementos from abandoned buildings and when I arrived home last summer with a handful of irises from an abandoned state school for the developmentally disabled she immediately cleared a spot in the yard for me to plant them. Though she had originally been doubtful they would survive, a few weeks ago she had looked outside to see them waving their bright purple beards proudly out in the yard.

"I'll take whatever. Since it's just an apartment I would rather take some of the new ones you planted that didn't come from somewhere special."

"That's fine. How's your writing coming?"

I shrugged. "Ok I guess. I haven't had a lot of time to work on it lately."

"Exploring with Luke a lot?" My mother loved Luke, as did my cat. He was just such a nice, easygoing guy that it was hard not to be won over almost instantly.

"Yeah. It's been a good summer for it. Oh, did I tell you I think I may have found a new teaching job for fall?"

She straightened and smiled. "No you didn't. I never understood why you left your job at the college....does this job pay better?"

"About the same. But it's younger kids. And I'd get to teach photography in their after school program."

"Well that's good then I guess. I wanted to show you this great lamp I found on eBay!" She bustled off to grab my father's laptop from the living room and commenced our regular show and tell. Her addiction to vintage items was almost as potent as my own.

After a few more hours of idle chitchat and cups of tea I packed up the cat and headed home where the apartment was bathed in the faint yellow glow of summer afternoon sun. The clouds that had hung over Pioneer Point had dispersed and there was a trail of pink across the sky, almost as if it was heralding the sunset, leading the sun in from the west.

I let the cat out of his carrier and locked the sliding door behind me. It was mercifully cool in the house so I settled in to watch TV but out of the corner of my eye that locked box seemed to be mocking me, taunting me. I tried putting it out of my line of sight but it was no use. That curiosity, the one that no doubt would someday kill me, was rearing its ugly head and pushing me to find out what was so important that someone had locked it away in this box and stashed it in the farthest corner under a bed.

Finally I sighed and pulled the box into my lap. It was about the size of a large sheet of paper and about five inches deep. It looked as if it had been painted a wonderful array of colors but they were now all chipped and faded, leaving only the ghost of an ornate floral design covering the entire thing. The lock was one of the old metal dials in which you had to line up the correct numbers in order to release the latch that held it closed which meant I had only two choices in opening this box: somehow find out the number required to release the latch, or break the box. I really didn't want to break it in order to get it open. Aside from being an object of intense curiosity it was also a beautiful antique in and of itself. I would have hated to damage it in any way. I picked it up from the table and shook it, though I'm not sure why. It wasn't as if that was going to accomplish much other than rattling the contents about and perhaps breaking things inside.

There were three dials, each most likely having nine digits apiece. I may have been terrible at math but even I knew that resulted in an innumerable amount of possible combinations to try, making the probability that I would stumble on the correct one rather *im*probable. I stretched out on the couch and propped the box on my stomach so that the dials were at eye level. If I knew who the box belonged to perhaps I could find out more about that person and eventually make an educated guess at the necessary combination of numbers but I had no way of knowing who the box belonged to as I wasn't even certain how long it had been there. For all I knew it was simply an antique that one of the boarders had stashed.

The dials were fairly tarnished, the silver patina having worn to an almost yellow glow. I tinkered with it, trying some of the more obvious combinations of numbers such as 1,2,3 and 4,5,6, hoping to hear the click of a catch releasing somewhere inside the box but the only response to my fiddling was the faint grind and squeak of the dials turning. I knew I wasn't going to get it open by guessing but every so often I looked away from the television and tried another combination, still with no success. Eventually I could feel myself dozing off, the box still resting on my stomach. I let my eyes close, not having realized I was still so tired, and allowed myself to take a nap. As I slept I dreamed of Green Gables as it once was, before it became a rooming house, before the additions. In my dream the cottage was warm and cozy, freshly painted with a fire going in each hearth. The little girl from the photo was also present in my dream, sitting on the living room floor with the doll. Somewhere in my dream state though I was bothered by a persistent squeak. I slowly opened my eyes just as the squeak gave way to a loud click and the box popped open.

I sat up and dropped the box on the floor, spilling its contents in every direction, watching the items scatter under the coffee table and across the rug. Sitting on the couch hugging my knees, I looked down at the pile of debris closest to my feet and saw that there were more photographs along with packets of folded papers tied with brown twine. There were also clumps of what looked like hair fastened with different colored bows. I sunk down to the floor and began gathering the contents of the box, piling it all on the surface of the coffee table. The photos were of little girls and the clumps of hair were actually carefully shorn locks of hair, lovingly wrapped in coils and secured with ribbon.

The box itself had tipped over and when I picked it up I found that there was also a bundle of newspaper clippings. They were yellowed and tattered, falling apart at the edges so I very carefully untied and unfolded each clipping. As I looked over them briefly I noticed that each article was accompanied by a photo-- photos of each of the little girls from the other photos in the box. It took nothing more than a quick skim of the articles to realize that I was not holding a memory box like I had thought.

Instead I had stumbled on something far more sinister and heinous: a murder box.

Chapter 9

A Sears truck was parked outside the Hollings house on Blackbird Road and Jim Hollings was shooting the breeze with the delivery man who had just dropped off his new riding mower. His youngest child, Nicole, came barreling out of the house, her long brown hair blowing behind her, a grass stain already streaked across her left knee.

"Daddy, daddy! Can I go over Lisbeth's?"

Hollings looked down at the seven year old with her big green eyes and smiled. "Of course sweetie. Be home by dinner."

He watched his daughter zig-zag through the backyard and onto the path that led through the woods to their nearest neighbor, the Carons. Their daughter Lisbeth, also seven, had become Nicole's favorite playmate. Jim never worried about Nicole crossing through the woods. The path was clearcut from years of neighbors using it to cross to the few houses that sat on the tiny dead end street running parallel to Blackbird Road. Nicky turned at the edge of the path and waved to her father, a big shining white smile on her face.

The Sears guy reached out to shake Jim's hand and climbed up onto his truck. That was Hollings' cue to hop on his new mower and try it out but he'd be damned if he was going to take it down to the Murray place again. He ran inside to grab a beer and settled himself on his new toy, humming as he mowed the grass that had barely even had a chance to grow after the last time he mowed but that hardly mattered to Jim Hollings. Mowing was his private time, as much as he loved his wife and kids.

A few hours later he had not only mowed the lawn but had hosed down the mower deck, emptied and cleaned the bagger, and rearranged the storage shed where the mower was kept. It was starting to approach dusk and he could see his wife in the kitchen getting dinner together. Linda looked up and smiled at her husband, then returned to her work. Jim turned and scanned the woods, wondering if Nicky had left the Caron's house yet, but it was still far too early to worry about her. She still had at least half an hour until their usual dinnertime.

Hollings didn't officially start to worry until he had gone inside to see Linda setting the table. His son, Robert had come in from biking to help Linda serve. It wasn't like Nicole to be this late.

"I'm going to run over to Sean and Cindy's. Nicky must have lost track of time."

"Ok honey. The chili will wait." She smiled and patted her husband's arm as he headed for the back door.

Jim stepped onto the path and walked quickly through the woods, trying to get to the Carons' as quickly as possible so that he wouldn't be walking Nicky home through the woods in the dark. He opened the gate that separated the Carons' yard from the woods and knocked on their back door. Cindy came to the screen with a puzzled look on her face.

"Hey Jim. What's up?"

"Hey Cindy. I just came to get Nicole."

"Jim, Nicky left an hour ago."

Chapter 10

After recovering my senses I started to read each article word for word. In all thirteen girls between the ages of seven and eleven years old had been taken from Blackbird Road and its surrounding neighborhoods. One girl each year from 1966 to

1979. The articles stopped in 1979 when the house was sold and converted to a rooming house. Every photo, every lock of hair matched the girls in the articles. I carefully tied the piles back together and packed everything back into the box, then threw it outside. There was no way in hell I wanted something like that in my house.

I jumped a mile when my cell phone vibrated in my pocket. The caller ID flashed-- Luke was calling. "You're not going to believe what's inside that box," I blundered the moment the call connected.

"Abby, there's a little girl missing from Blackbird Road. Her father's riding mower was set on fire in the backyard of Green Gables."

I sat down hard on the deck, the box lying on its side in the corner near the railing. "That's what the scorch marks were from...Luke that box is full of serial killer trophies. From a child killer."

"What? Are you kidding?" Luke fell silent. I sat with my eyes closed, my forehead perched in my left hand, the phone clutched in my right.

"What the hell did we stumble into this time?" I sighed.

"Looks like we found a murderer. I'm on my way over. We need to turn this over to the police and forget Green Gables exists."

He disconnected and I stayed where I was, staring at the box. I considered what the implications would be if we admitted to having been in the house and finding that box. We were trespassing, we were present when an inordinate amount of damage had been done to both the house and the barn, and we had broken through the lawn in order to escape from the tunnel. Admitting any of that to the police could have quite unfavorable consequences for us. However, not turning over the box could be even worse.

Luke came up the stairs to find me in the same spot, my head spinning. He bent to pick up the box and opened it, looking inside but touching nothing. "This is disgusting."

"I know. I can't believe how easily trouble finds me. I need to stop picking things up in abandoned buildings." I tried to say it with a bit of humor but I couldn't muster it.

"Ok we need to turn this in to the police but we need to decide how we are going to do this.." Luke sighed and pinched the bridge of his nose, a sure sign that he was starting a headache. "We can consider dropping it off anonymously but if any of those cop shows are at all accurate they'll dust that thing for fingerprints which means they'll find us eventually since we touched it. We'll automatically be suspects with little chance to explain ourselves. The second option is to turn it in and find the best way to explain how we got it without implicating ourselves in a number of other crimes like trespass and destruction of property."

I thought for a moment but the answer was clear. "Let's just be smart about it and bring it in. But that means burning the explore. We can't ever go back."

"Then that's what we have to do. I would rather not be mixed up in this, especially since there is now a girl missing. It could all tie together and I want nothing to do with it."

"Agreed." I thought again for a moment though, thinking I wanted to visit the house one more time before going to the police. I wanted to see if the little girl appeared again. "Let's do this...I want to visit the house one more time. If we can do that, then we'll go to the police immediately after."

Luke threw back his head and laughed. "How did I know you were going to say that?"

"Because you know me well. Can we do it?"

Luke sighed. "Yeah we can do it. It's still early enough so let's roll."

We didn't say much on our way to the house. I stared out the window, thinking about the box and the little girl that was missing. I knew I was getting ahead of myself but in my head I was already trying to connect the past murders to yesterday's disappearance. Could it possibly be the same person? And what about the apparition? Who was she? Was she also a victim even though she didn't appear in the box? Her clothing was also from a much earlier period than that of the other girls. There was nothing on the surface that seemed to connect her to the others but my gut told me she was indeed somehow linked to them.

We were forced to park in the layby again but this time because there was caution tape threaded through the trees and across both paths leading to the house. There was no choice but to thread our way through the woods at the back of the house. It was a much longer route to the rear of the cottage, branches hitting us in the face, tearing at our clothes and hair. We finally made it to the window and hoisted ourselves into the pantry. Everything looked as it had the last time we left the house, which was a strange sort of comfort, knowing the cottage hadn't been disturbed, though I would have thought the police would have had to search here for the girl.

"Ah they have been in here," Luke whispered, pointing to the kitchen window, which was now boarded up, the table pushed to the side. In the living room the shades were still drawn but the windows that had been blown out by the storm were also boarded up, the glass swept into piles below the windowsill. We moved methodically through each room, noting the changes throughout the house. The door leading from the house to the barn was also boarded up and fresh caution tape was strung across. The upstairs was largely untouched though there were some signs of a search-- closets were opened, their contents scattered on the floor, beds pushed away to be sure there was no one hidden underneath-- but otherwise the second floor looked exactly the same. Luke headed into the master bedroom but I hooked a left and headed for the child's room. The bed there had also been moved though there certainly was not enough room to hide below it. I gingerly pushed the bed back into the corner and sat on the soiled mattress, closing my eyes to think. When I opened them again I was no longer alone.

The little girl was seated on the bed next to me, her hands folded in her lap. She looked up at me but didn't smile, fear clouding her nearly transparent eyes. "He took her."

"Took who?" My heart raced as the little girl reached out her tiny hand and let it hover above my arm, making all the hairs on my arm stand straight up. The apparition looked over her shoulder, startled by a noise behind her, and faded away. Moments later Luke joined me, sitting on the bed where the girl had been. "Satisfied?" he asked, patting my knee.

I nodded. "Yeah. There's nothing to see here."

We moved slowly back down the stairs and out the door, collecting ourselves before heading to the New Salem Police. I sat in the front seat of the car and held the box in my lap, attempting to concoct what I believed to be a plausible explanation of how we came across the box. Unfortunately nothing I came up with sounded even remotely realistic and I was confronted with the realization that Luke and I would simply have to admit to having been in the house. The police station wasn't far away but the ride was long enough for my heart to climb into my throat. We both dragged our feet across the parking lot and into the building where I realized I had lost all power of speech. Luke stepped up to the counter and asked for the officer in charge of the missing Hollings girl. I never saw a police department mobilize so quickly in my life.

A young, good-looking detective in a tailored gray suit led us to a desk, looking us over suspiciously as we sat, the box sitting in my lap. I glanced over at Luke to see that he too was trying to work out how to explain the box and its contents when the detective jumped in.

"What have you got there?"

I lifted the box onto the detective's desk and pushed it toward him. "We found this in the yard of a house on Blackbird Road."

"And?" He gestured at me to keep talking, lifting an eyebrow at me as he so obviously wondered what was wrong with the two of us.

"Well, it's filled with newspaper clippings and other...items...that seem to be connected to the disappearance of a number of girls who were kidnapped and murdered in the 1970's."

The detective, whose nameplate I noticed said Benson, reached out and pulled the box closer. He popped it open, slowly removing the contents and examining each piece carefully. "These are all from a cold case back in the 70's. There was no evidence in the original case except the bodies." He was all but talking to himself as he arranged the locks of hair and other items into neat piles. "Looks like the original detective on the case was right. It was a serial killer." Though his voice showed little emotion as he spoke, his face was a mask of anger and sadness. "Where did you say you found this?"

Luke and I looked at each other, wondering how much to tell him. I decided to take a chance and explain everything. "We...rather I found it under a bed in the cottage of a farm on Blackbird Road. I'm pretty sure it was a child's bedroom."

Detective Benson sighed and closed the box. "Under the circumstances I'm not going to ask what you were doing inside the house because that's not my concern right now. What else can you tell me?"

"We were inside taking photographs. That's what we do. I found the box but we saw nothing else." I hesitated again, but it occurred to me that the tunnels could be important. They would be the perfect place to conceal a frightened little girl. "The house has tunnels. From what we saw they go all the way out to the woods. They were slave tunnels at one time."

"Tunnels?" Benson looked puzzled until I explained about the research I had done on the house. "And you said you took photos?"

I nodded and reached down to pull my camera out of my bag, glad I had decided at the last minute to bring it in with me. I stood and came around the detective's desk to show him the photos.

"I know this house. The Murray Farm. It was the late 60's when little girls started going missing from neighboring towns. They had a lead back then but it was flimsy at best."

"How many girls in all?" I asked.

Detective Benson thought for a second. "Thirteen. Looks like they're all in that box you found." He sighed and shook his head, looking suddenly quite tired. "You know I'm going to tell you both to stay away from that house. Looks like my people will be needing to get in there and you're going to have to explain how to get to these tunnels."

An hour later we had explained how to find the tunnels from the backyard and I drew him a crude map of the property. "I'll need you both to leave your contact information in case I have more questions."

With a shaky hand I wrote down my name, number, and address. He warned us again to stay away from the house but luckily he said nothing about us having been in the house illegally. We thanked him and left the police station before he could change his mind, then climbed in the hot car to head home.

"So it sounds like the detective sees the same connection between those other girls and the one that's missing now."

Luke looked distressed by that idea and truth be told, so was I. That meant it was possible there was some sort of elderly serial killer on the loose, or it could mean someone had suddenly decided to pick up where the other killer left off. Of course that was all speculation at the moment, as no one actually knew whether or not Nicole Hollings was still alive.

"Thirteen girls," he said, shaking his head and gripping the steering wheel. "What the hell did we get ourselves into this time?"

I stared out the window as we wound our way down Route 202 towards home. "I don't know but I'm going to be optimistic and hope that what we just gave the police will help them find that other little girl before she gets hurt."

Or worse.

***

By the time I got home I felt good about what we had done. It was smart to turn that box over to Detective Benson and it would be even smarter to steer clear of the Murray Farm even though it would be difficult to control my curiosity. After digging into the strangeness at Westwood Asylum I found that my natural penchant for a good mystery could certainly get me into trouble but this time the police were involved, as was a living, breathing little girl who was most likely scared out of her wits. This wasn't like Westwood at all.

I put on the teakettle and bent to pet Riley who was winding himself around my ankles, looking cute as ever. "Yes, yes. I know you want to eat and I will feed you in a minute." The cat stopped winding and sat down, tucking his tail in front of his paws and blinking up at me just in case I had missed the cute he was putting out a moment before. I stood to pour my tea first then turned to grab the cat's food container off the top of the refrigerator. I put it up that high after I found that Riley had an uncanny ability to open his container and self-serve. He woke me up one night banging around my bedroom and when I turned on the light I found him wandering around with the cover of his food container stuck around his neck. Apparently jamming his head into the container to gorge himself hadn't worked out quite as he had planned.

Leaning against the counter I sipped my tea and went over the day's events in my head, happy to no longer have that disturbing box anywhere near me. Outside I could hear the sounds of birds in the trees and kids playing on the playground in the center of town, only a few blocks away. They were comforting sounds, sounds that reminded me that I was safer in my own home than traipsing around in an abandoned house.

I turned away from the door and headed into the living room, slipping off my shoes as I went. It was hot, slightly stuffy in the house but it was one of those days when I didn't really mind. All I would have to do was open a window in each room and a perfect cross breeze would pick up through the apartment. As I moved into the living room I stopped to grab the copy of *Anne of Green Gables* that I had picked up n the Murray house, then sat on the couch pulling out the photo of the little girl.

"I'm going to call you Anne." I said out loud to the tiny face in the picture. I turned the photo over in my hands, again looking for any kind of marking or label but there was none. "What's your story Anne? What happened to you?" *And why was I able to see you in the house?*

I nearly jumped out of my skin when I heard a knock on my slider. I dropped the photo and it slid under the couch, my tea sloshing over the edge of the mug and onto the coffee table. Most of my friends knew I wasn't fond of surprise visits and therefor called ahead. Door to door salesmen and the like didn't generally climb the back stairs to the third floor to hock their wares so I approached the kitchen carefully, hugging the wall in the hallway so I could perhaps get a glimpse of who was on my porch before making myself seen. That was the biggest drawback to having floor to ceiling glass in the kitchen. It made me awfully vulnerable. I peeked carefully around the corner and was relieved to find that it was Detective Benson at my door.

"Detective. You scared me. Come on in." I pulled the slider open and motioned for him to step into the kitchen. He looked around at the kitchen, his gaze settling on the slider.

"You should keep that thing locked. And covered. Anyone can see into this place."

I nodded and smiled, laughing a bit at how intense he sounded. "I know, I was just thinking about that for the hundredth time. I did however install an alarm on it so that's something. What can I do for you?"

"I sent a few of my guys over to the Murray farm. They followed your instructions and found the hole in the yard. Unfortunately the tunnels were empty except for a couple of chairs. And of course footprints from you and your friend there."

"In other words, nothing you could use to find the Hollings girl."

"No ma'am. I also did a little digging into the cold cases. There wasn't much more than what was reported in the papers but the original suspect was a man named Roma. Anthony Roma. Lived diagonally behind the Murray farm. Apparently there are a number of paths through the woods that lead from the houses on Blackbird Road to the ones on the next street over, though there weren't nearly as many houses on either street back then." The detective leaned back against the only wall that didn't have cabinets and crossed his arms over his chest, taking in the rest of my closet-sized kitchen. "How do you cook in here?"

I threw my head back and laughed. "Very carefully. It's a challenge sometimes in a room this small. Needless to say I wash all my dishes the moment I use them. There isn't enough space to leave a pile of dirty bowls and such." As I talked Riley appeared out of nowhere and looked up at Benson, curiosity and mischief in his eyes. Before I could catch him he wound himself around the detective's ankles and let out a rather demanding yowl. "I'm so sorry, God I hope you like cats. He's very pushy with newcomers."
He laughed and bent down to pet Riley on his fuzzy gray head. "He's cute." Riley threw himself on the floor and rolled over to have his tummy pet. "And fat. I don't think I've ever seen a cat this large before."

"Yeah he's a bit of a chubber." I watched him for a moment until I suddenly remembered my manners. "Can I get you something? A cup of tea? Soda? Water?"

Benson straightened back up and thought for a moment, his eyes going to the teakettle. "Tea would be fine thank you. I actually have a few more questions for you about the house and where you found that box."

"Sure. Not a problem." I turned the kettle back on and went to grab my own mug from the living room where the tea I spilled had already stained the top of the table. Thankfully it wasn't a piece I particularly cared for. Something I had inherited from an ex. I found the detective staring at a framed photo of the Worcester State Hospital that I had hanging next to the doorway leading into the hallway.

"This is beautiful. Did you take that?"

I nodded. "It's the administration building of Worcester State Hospital here in Massachusetts."

"An insane asylum?" He turned to stare at me, his eyebrows drawn tight in a frown. "Why on earth would you take photos of something like that?"

If only I had a nickel for every time someone asked me that question. "Well, they're beautiful when you know their history."

"I do know their history. They were snake pits. Horror films in the making."

I shook my head and motioned for him to follow me into the hallway where the walls were lined with more photos and shelves full of the bits and pieces I had collected over the years. "Look at these." I pointed to a collection of vintage postcards that showed some of the asylums in their heyday. "They were beautifully constructed palaces that were meant to heal. You have to know their *real* history. They started out..." I looked up at the detective and realized I was babbling. Or rather lecturing, a habit that I sometimes had a difficult time curtailing. "Sorry. I'm sure you don't want to hear all this."

Benson immediately held out his hand as if to grab my elbow but stopped short. "No, no. It sounds like you know quite a bit about these places. How did you ever start photographing places like this?" He moved down the line looking closely at each collection of photos, and then moved on to the collections of letterhead, state hospital stickers, and other paper items that were mounted and framed together with the individual photos. "It's like a museum in here."

"I have a friend, Helen, who frequently jokes that I should hire her as a docent to guide visitors through my collection." I reached past him and pointed to a photo of Northampton State Hospital, the first building I ever explored. "I used to teach in a facility that housed children with mental illness. It was an old building that had been an orphanage in the 1800's. I got curious about the history of the place and found out it had ties to Northampton State Hospital a half hour north and the hospital was going to be torn down. I convinced a friend to go see it with me. We drove around the town for a while before we found it but when we finally did...it was amazing. Just sitting there up on a hill. By then a private developer had bought the old hospital and was getting ready to tear it down so it was fenced in but one of the buildings on the edge of the property was open."

I laughed and shook my head at the memory, then looked over to see that the detective was actually listening intently to my story, waiting for me to finish.

"My friend was afraid. He didn't want to go in but there were these kids who couldn't have been more than 16. They said they knew their way through the tunnels and were willing to show us how to get into the building. I remember walking into those tunnels for the first time and thinking how strange it was to be underground like that. That was before I knew that the hospital used to use those tunnels to move patients around."

"It sounds like there's a lot to learn about these places."

"There definitely is. There's so much more to them than people realize." I suddenly felt embarrassed for going on the way I did. "You said you had more questions about the house."

He looked surprised, like he had forgotten he'd said that. "Ah yes. Yes I do. Is there somewhere we can sit down?"

"Of course." I led the way to the living room and sat, Detective Benson taking the other end of the couch.

"Why the Murray farm?"

"Pardon?"

"You said you were there to take pictures and I see now that you do a lot of that, breaking into places."

I cringed at his use of the term "breaking in" though that was obviously what I did. It just sounded different coming from someone who held the authority of the law. "I photograph anything architectural to be honest."

"Yet I don't see any photos of...nice buildings, shall we say." He looked around the living room where the walls were adorned with even more photos of peeling paint and decaying wood.

"Yes, I focus on abandoned buildings. I'm a history buff and I like photographing the things people leave behind. I heard about the Murray house from a friend who had also photographed it and Luke and I-- that's the guy I had with me today-- decided to see it for ourselves."

"How did you get in?"

"There was a rotted board on one of the back windows. We climbed in that way."

"Was there any sign that others had done the same?"

I thought for a moment, wondering how to explain exploration to him without giving away too much. "Of course there were signs."

"What signs? How do you know they were signs?"

"When you've been an explorer as long as I have you just know the signs."

Picking up his mug and lifting it to his lips, Detective Benson watched me for a moment, unnerving me slightly with his studied gaze. "What is an explorer?"

"It's what you call someone who does what I do. With the buildings." I took a sip of my tea and sat back into the cushions. "When we got into the house I could see where other photographers had set up shots, like moving a chair or arranging a pile of books just so. You could also see where people had sat on the beds and even stood in the bathtub. The signs aren't hard to miss."

The detective also sat back and took a sip of his own tea. "So you weren't the first one to break in for what seem like fairly benign reasons. What did you find in the house?"

"Well, everything really."

"What do you mean everything?"

"I mean everything. The house looks as if life just stopped in there one day. Beds were still made. There were books left open on nightstands, clothes still hanging in the closets. Someone had even left their notebooks from a college course out in the sitting room as if they had been studying and got up to do something. They just never came back."

"I gather it was a rooming house for a number of years after the Murray family died out. How did you find out about the tunnels?"

"Completely by accident actually. We were under the barn and the floor above us collapsed. The only way to safety was through a door that led to the tunnels."

"How did you know they were slave tunnels?"

"I didn't until I did some research about the area." There was no way I was going to tell him about Mary Ellen doing a deed search for me. There were some secrets I didn't feel the need to disclose.

"Well, like I said, we didn't find anything that could help us with the Hollings girl. Not that I expected to find her hidden down there or anything but I had hoped there would at least be some evidence somewhere. Oh well. Abigail, thank you for the information."

"You're very welcome. And please, call me Abby."

He smiled, a nice wide smile that reached right to his blue eyes. "Abby. You can call me Chris. Thanks again for your help." He reached out and shook my hand, then stood and headed for the kitchen. I followed him in and watched as he carefully set his mug in the sink and stopped to pat Riley once more before heading out the door. I looked down at my hand for a moment, thinking it was still warm from his grip. Pleasantly warm.

Chapter 11

Jim and Linda Hollings sat at their kitchen table, shock and fear radiating from them both as Linda's sister, Renee buzzed around making dinner for her nephew because she knew that Linda and Jim wouldn't eat. They hadn't eaten since Nicole had gone missing no matter how Renee had badgered them. Today she simply went about her business and cooked enough for her and Robert, ignoring her sister's protestations that she didn't need to bother. It almost seemed as if Linda had forgotten she had another child.

Jim sat with a beer in his hand but he didn't drink it, just pushed it back and forth across the table from palm to palm, occasionally looking up to glance out the window as if he expected his daughter to come bounding across the backyard. Linda on the other hand seemed to be avoiding looking out the window.

The police had been in and out of the Hollings' home almost every day for the past week but still no one seemed to have any idea where Nicole had gone. They knew she had left the Carons' house around 5:30 that day but beyond that... Linda had overheard one young officer say it seemed almost as if she had disappeared off the face of the earth without a trace. She had wondered about that. How does one disappear without a trace? Was her daughter sucked up by aliens? Vaporized somehow? Sometimes when she felt herself coming apart at the seams a bit she would think about that and find that she was actually mildly entertained by that thought.

Every day was the same now. The police came and updated the Hollings, such as they could, then the family "ate" dinner together at the table, such as it was. Jim then sat in the living room watching television and Linda stayed in her place at the table. It was summer so Robert was on vacation for another month but no one seemed to notice his comings and goings. After all, he was a boy. No one had to worry about a boy.

After a few weeks though the police stopped coming. Renee too spent fewer hours with her sister's family, mostly because she could no longer watch her sister ignore the remainder of her life. Renee didn't have kids so she acknowledged that she had no idea what it might feel like to have one of them taken away but she also couldn't understand how her sister could just give up hope. She had overheard the same statement that Nicky hadn't left a trace. Unlike Linda, Renee thought that was a good sign. That meant Nicky didn't struggle. It meant she wasn't hurt when she was taken. Maybe she even knew the person who had taken her. She knew that was a strange way to look at things but she refused to give up hope that her niece would turn up unscathed.

"I'm going to head home Linda." Renee put the last of the clean dishes in the cabinet and hung the dishtowel on the handle of the oven. Linda barely acknowledged her, as usual. Renee shook her head and grabbed her purse then moved toward the front door.

"She's not coming back."

Renee stopped short, Linda's voice startling her. "Don't say that Linda."

"It's true. She's dead by now. It's been too long."

"No Linda. You can't think that way." Renee shook her head vehemently, knowing that arguing with her sister was a waste of time, but she couldn't help herself. "Nevermind," she whispered, opening the door and letting herself out, leaving Linda alone in the kitchen, still refusing to look out the window.

Chapter 12

It had been three weeks since Luke and I had turned in the box. Three weeks since Detective Benson had appeared on my doorstep. We had stayed away from the house, stayed away from exploring all together at the moment as Luke was in the middle of prepping for graduate school while working full time. I on the other hand rearranged my apartment at least once a week, haunted the antique shops in my neighborhood, and read as many trashy romance novels as I could get my hands on.

One Friday afternoon Riley and I sat under the window at the end of the hallway, a book lying in my lap while I watched the world go by outside. Riley purred with his eyes screwed shut, a giant kitty smile on his face as I stroked him absentmindedly. I began to feel my eyelids drooping when I noticed an unmarked police car pulling around the corner and into my driveway. I stood up, forgetting Riley was in my lap, dumping him onto the floor. He took off running down the hall but slid to a stop when he heard a knock on the slider. He turned abruptly and galloped into the kitchen, meowing at Detective Benson who stood outside the screen door waiting for me to open it.

"Detective...I mean Chris. How are you?" I felt myself smiling broadly at him, happy to see him.

"I'm well thank you Abby. How are you?"

"I'm well." I opened the screen and motioned Chris into the kitchen. "What can I do for you?"

"Well, I wanted to let you know that we still don't have any leads on the missing Hollings girl. Unfortunately it doesn't look as if that's going to change."

I frowned, thinking of the poor girl's family. "I'm sorry to hear that. That can't be easy for her parents."

"No I can't imagine it is. We see it a lot but as police officers we can only guess at what goes through their heads when we're investigating."

"I was just about to have a cup of tea. Would you like to join me?"

Chris nodded and smiled. I reached for the box of teabags and turned to see him reaching for the two mugs that were sitting in the dish drainer. I watched him set them carefully on the stove while I filled the kettle and set it to boil.

"So was that the only reason you came all the way out here? To give me a depressing update?" I said, smirking.

"Um...no actually...I..." For the first time Detective Benson looked a bit flustered. "Well, I wanted to see more of your photos."

Was he blushing? Watching him struggle to finish his sentence made me laugh out loud. "Ok. Sure. Let me finish making the tea and I'll give you the grand tour."

I poured the tea and handed him a cup, then led him back out to the hallway. "What do you want to see first?"

He looked around and zeroed in on a floor to ceiling bookshelf against the wall. "What is all this?"

"Well most of the books are mental health books but some of them are books that I have found in the buildings I explored."

Chris turned and looked at me with a twisted smile on his face. "So in other words they're things you've stolen?"

"Oh...well...I guess...."

"I'm teasing you. What are these?" He had picked up a pair of milk glass bottles with black caps.

"They're old lab bottles from a state school for the developmentally disabled."

"And this?" He put the bottles back down and grabbed a small cardboard box with blue lettering.

"That's a prescription box from the 1940's. It was something my grandmother saved."

"Hmm." He continued to look through the books and other pieces of paper then flicked through the basket of pamphlets and letterhead that I had collected from numerous state institutions over the years. "You have an interesting collection, that's for sure. Show me more."

I took him through the house and showed him the mirror from Westwood, the typewriter from Belchertown State School, the dishes from Monson Developmental Center. I even showed him Isabella Monteforte's diary, the patient who was murdered at Westwood, though I didn't explain to him exactly what it was. Finally we sat on the couch and I showed him the rest of my collection of vintage postcards. I collected cards for every building I had ever photographed, some of them quite rare and though it was sometimes tough to explain to people why I loved what I did, they often understood a little bit better after seeing how beautiful the buildings once were.

"You do have quite the passion for all this, don't you?"

I laughed and sat back on the couch, taking a sip of my tea. "I do. I love history and I love other peoples' stories. It makes the buildings come alive I guess."

"I guess I never thought of buildings as alive before. Though it certainly makes sense." He too laughed and relaxed into the couch cushions a bit. "I like you. You're different. Not like the other women who find themselves in a police station on a Saturday."

"Well that's because I'm not a prostitute."

Chris laughed loud and hard at that one, spilling a bit of his tea in his lap as his hand shook. "Very true. Very true indeed. Well Abby, unfortunately I have to go back to work." He cleared his throat and wiped at the puddle of lukewarm liquid he had spilled on his slacks. He stood and reached out to shake my hand again. "Do you think maybe you'd like to have dinner with me Friday night?"

He still had ahold of my hand and I realized my mouth was hanging open in surprise. Detective Benson had just asked me out. "Um, sure. I would love to," I said once I had regained my ability to speak.

"Isn't that something. Love to." He smiled wide. "I'll pick you up around 7:00."

"Sounds good." I nodded and slid the screen closed behind him, watching him retreat down the stairs. I couldn't believe I had just agreed to a date with Detective Benson. It had been a while since I had been on a first date. I had had a string of less than successful relationships the last couple of years and so had avoided any type of romantic entanglement since. I was perfectly happy hanging out with Luke and exploring, no strings attached and no expectations beyond getting into a building. We had become so comfortable with each other that there was no longer any such thing as an awkward silence. Neither one of us ever felt the need to push conversation or entertain the other. At times that was the hardest part about dating. I had always felt pressed to keep the conversation moving which usually led to nonsensical babbling or unnecessary preaching.

I had also found it difficult to explain my obsession with abandoned buildings to members of the opposite sex. Once on a second date I was told that if he and I were to continue to see each other I would have to stop exploring. The young man whom I had only been to dinner with once before informed me that it wasn't an acceptable hobby for a woman to undertake, especially any woman who would be dating him. After all, he had an image to maintain. It's funny-- I never saw him again...

 Though our dinner date was still a few days away I found that I was already nervous. What should I wear? What would we talk about? Would we just talk about the Hollings girl and exploring, then lapse into silence? My worst nightmare was that we wouldn't have anything to talk about.

Thankfully my fears were unfounded. I wore a simple outfit of jeans; a white ruffled short-sleeved blouse, and comfortable shoes. I tucked a sweater in my purse in case we were going somewhere with extra powerful air conditioning. Chris picked me up promptly at 7:00 and wound up taking me to Spoletto, one of my favorite restaurants. We sat drinking wine and talking about our jobs, our families, and our hobbies. We laughed through our meals and shared dessert, suddenly realizing that it was almost 11:00 pm.

"Time flies," Chris said, emptying his wine glass. "Shall we?" He flipped the bill over and looked at it discreetly, then slid it back onto the table with his credit card on top. I too reached for the bill but he stopped me with a gentle hand. "My treat. I asked you out remember?"

I blushed, afraid I had perhaps offended him but then I could see he was smiling. "It's habit. Luke and I split everything when we go out."

"Yes but Luke is your friend. I on the hand am your knight in shining armor. At least for tonight."

"So chivalry is not dead after all I see."

"Not here it's not." Chris and I walked out to the parking lot where he even went so far as to open my car door for me.

"Why thank you sir. I feel like such a lady tonight!"

"As well you should," he laughed. "I wouldn't want you to have dressed up for nothing!"

Chris and I even continued to chat on the drive back to my apartment and without even a second thought I invited him up for a cup of tea. He however politely declined. "Unfortunately I have to work tomorrow. With the Hollings girl still missing we've been clocking quite a bit of overtime. I'll take a rain check though." He came around to my side of the car to open the door for me, then leaned down and gave me a kiss on the cheek. "Thank you for having dinner with me. I had a great time."

"So did I. Thank you for inviting me."

"We'll have to do it again. Soon. Good night."

"Good night."

I went to bed that night on cloud nine. It had been a long time since I had been on such a successful first date that it made me dare to hope the second would be as good. The next morning I awoke ready to enjoy the day, beginning with a cup of tea and some time in front of the computer looking over my photos from the Murray Farm. The outside of the house was so choked with flowering vines that many of the photos I had taken had a thick green haze over them. Normally I would consider the photos ruined by such a strong colorcast but instead the tinted fog just increased the feeling of magic in the frames.

My favorite so far was a photo I had taken of the front door. It was taken from a low angle in order to show the lovely arbor that arched over the small cement stoop. Built into the arbor were two little green bench seats that looked cozy and charming against the peeling white paint of the arbor. The door itself was painted the same green as the benches and so were the shutters on each window. Though the clapboard siding was actually white, the hunter green leaves on the arbor made the house look earthy with a sort of ethereal glow. I could almost imagine the little girl from the photo in the book playing out on that porch, sitting on one of the benches imagining her day away. But then I could also imagine her being taken from that porch, kidnapped and hidden away from her parents. It was a heartbreaking thought.

Looking through the remainder of the photos I wondered if I would see her, the little girl I had chosen to call Anne, but there was nothing in the photos that shouldn't have been. After everything that had happened at Westwood maybe I had been imagining the specter I had seen in the Murray cottage. I suppose that was quite possible.

A few hours later I finished editing most of the photos and was happy with what I had gotten this time. They were all in focus, all well lit and I was pleased with the composition. All in all I thought it had been a successful trip. I shut down my computer and went to grab some laundry, dragging it down to the basement to throw it in. The basement was about ten degrees cooler than my apartment but it was still slightly dirty and musty so it wasn't a place I really wanted to hang out for any length of time though it was far better than the laundromat down the street that was always clogged with kids from the private school up on the hill. Private school kids were a breed all their own. They were loud, they were rude, and they had no problem taking your laundry out of a machine and leaving it on the floor if they wanted the machine. At least in my dirty musty basement I knew I could walk away from my laundry and not worry about losing it.

I went back upstairs and picked up the book I had been reading the day before and curled up in the window. Before I could even focus on the page Riley had already hopped up in my lap and started to purr. I put the book down and used both hands to stroke his soft gray fur, watching as his eyes narrowed to happy slits, his cheeks puffing out with each purr he exhaled. The heat and humidity that floated through the window and enveloped me made me sleepy, my eyelids drooping. Soon the cat and I were both asleep.

Chapter 13

Luke called that Saturday morning sounding excited. "Look I know I'm not usually the one to suggest things like this but I heard they took the police tape down at Green Gables. They didn't find anything there so it's fair game again. I kind of want to go back and see more of that tunnel."

"Wow that is a first!" I laughed quite hard at that, as Luke was usually the hyper cautious one. "I don't see why not. I'd love to see how far that tunnel goes."

"Ok good because I'm already pulling in your driveway."

Luke bounded up the stairs and into the apartment. He sat on the floor and petted Riley while he waited for me to gather up my camera bag and put my hair up. I was ready in record time and hopped in the car with Luke.

It was even hotter out that day than it was the last time we went to the house. I started to sweat the moment I stepped out of my apartment and was glad I had decided to wear a tank top rather than a t-shirt. I stuck my head out the window as we drove up Route 202 into New Salem. Occasionally the winding road was actually cool and comfortable, the trees' leaves thick and lush, reaching from each side of the road and touching in the middle. Every so often when I looked far enough out the passenger side window I could see glimpses of the Quabbin Reservoir laying low behind the trees. It was such a beautiful piece of water but it was cloaked in so many dark and disturbing stories. According to some when the water is low enough you can see the spire from the old Enfield church sticking up from the glassy surface. Others say there are places where railroad tracks plummet into the water, going nowhere. Once they began allowing divers in the water the stories multiplied. Divers claimed there were still hundreds of buildings below, saying it reminded them of the mining town in *Silent Hill*. Of course historical records refuted those claims, showing how the towns had been demolished, cemeteries moved, factories dismantled long before the area was flooded. Still, it was an enchanting place with so much "scope for the imagination" as Anne Shirley would say.

Luke pulled slowly onto Blackbird Road and coasted by the house, making certain the police tape was truly gone and that the house was indeed quiet. I could almost imagine the house watching us pass by as we turned around and circled back to park in the layby, not wanting to take a chance parking in the yard. I wasn't sure that my dinner date with Detective Benson would earn me any kind of leniency if we were to get caught on the property.

"I don't know what it is about this place," Luke said, looking up into the gables where the shades were drawn tightly. "There's something about it that makes me want to come back over and over again. Sometimes I think I wouldn't mind coming here just to look, never mind take photos."

"This house certainly does seem to have a life of its own. I feel like it watches us when we're here. I know that sounds strange..."

Luke laughed and shook his head. "After everything that happened at Westwood I don't find much strange anymore."

"You have a point. Though I believe Westwood was a somewhat unique experience. I had a concrete tie to both Isabella *and* the hospital. I'm not sure that could ever happen again like that. Though I really don't know. I never would have expected to happen even once. But I have to be honest, the last time we were here, just before I found that box, I'm pretty sure there was a little girl sitting next to me on that bed."

Stopping short in front of the cottage Luke looked at me, his eyes wide, his mouth frozen in a bit of a grimace. "Why didn't you tell me that before?"

"To be honest I firmly believe I imagined her. Sometimes I forget how terrible the fire at Westwood was and how difficult it was to lose Cameron. I didn't really take much time to think about it after it happened so the fact that I'm exploring again...well I suppose it just triggered some of the leftover stress."

Luke slung his arm over my shoulders and gave me a quick squeeze. "Man I never really thought of t that way. I guess that was pretty stressful."

"It is what it is. It's over and here we are! In the middle of another bizarre mystery. Thankfully this time the police are involved and no one is looking at me like I'm crazy!"

We both laughed and wandered slowly towards the back of the house, taking our time, not worried about being seen as there hadn't been another car on the road for the last half hour.

Unfortunately we quickly discovered that the pantry window had been boarded up with new plywood and heavy carriage bolts. There was no way we were getting in that way. I shielded my eyes from the sun and looked around, wondering how we were going to get in until I had an idea.

"Why don't we just uncover the hole we made in the roof of the tunnel? We can just drop into the tunnel and follow it down."

"I have an even better idea." Luke disappeared around the front of the house. I listened hard until I heard the squeak of the barn door being dragged open. A few minutes later Luke came back around the corner of the cottage with a wooden ladder in his hand. "Now we can get in and out of that tunnel without breaking our necks."

"Brilliant!" I helped him uncover the hole in the tunnel and we lowered the ladder until it rested firmly on the floor in the dark below. Luke scrambled down the rickety ladder and jiggled it around until the base was a bit more secure. I made sure my backpack was tight over my shoulder and turned to lower myself down the ladder and into the tunnel.

We waited to let our eyes adjust to the blackness before pulling out our flashlights. I scanned the walls and ceiling with my flashlight, wondering at the level of ingenuity that went into building the tunnels. There were also little recesses in the walls that at a guess most likely held jugs of water or packets of food at one time. There wasn't much else besides dirt clinging to every surface and the one lone wooden chair we had left there the last time we had been in the tunnel. We turned and bravely headed down the tunnel towards Quabbin. I swept my flashlight from side to side, hoping to find something left behind but there was nothing. It was clear that the tunnel had not been disturbed for quite some time.

Or so we thought.

A few hundred feet into the tunnel my flashlight caught on a shadow in the dirt that coated the floor and it was immediately clear to me that it was a footprint. There was also no doubt that the footsteps were made by modern day shoes. Someone else had been in that tunnel and they had been there fairly recently as the print had barely filled in with fresh dust.

I put out an arm to stop Luke from stepping through the print and pointed it out to him. "Someone has been down here. Recently."

He bent to look closer at the print, pulling out his camera and taking a quick snap of the footprint. "I guess that means once again we need to get out of here and get this to the police. Again."

"We can't win with this place. We'll never see the rest of this tunnel after we turn this over."

"There's nothing we can do about it. This might help their case in finding that girl."

I sighed and turned back in the direction of the ladder. Back on the surface the sun had intensified, the heat shimmering around us as we climbed up out of the tunnel. I got to the top of the ladder a few steps behind Luke and as I looked up to see how far I had to go I was startled when I saw the heat shimmer take shape in front of me into the little girl from the photo. I jumped a mile and lost my grip on the ladder, then went tumbling back down to earth, hitting the dirt floor hard, hard enough that I knew I was going to lose consciousness. Lying on the dirt, I watched the dust settle around me as my eyesight blurred, the little girl bent over me, her body filling in and becoming clearer as my eyesight grew dimmer.

"Don't tell him..." She reached out to touch me just as I blacked out.

***

I woke to the glaring bright lights of a hospital emergency room, Luke parked in a chair next to the bed, an IV snaking its way from the back of my hand.

"Dude, what the hell happened?"

Luke picked his head up from his hands and smiled at me. "Dude, you fell down the ladder."

"Oh God. Did I really?" I tried to bring my head to my forehead but I was tethered to about a hundred beeping machines. My other arm appeared to be in a cast. "Shit, did I break my arm?"

"Um no. The cast is just decoration," Luke said with a smirk. "Yeah you broke it. But the doctor said it wasn't too bad of a break."

I was about to ask a few more questions when the curtain surrounding my bed parted and Chris Benson walked in. "So I hear you had a bit of a spill."

Hanging my head, I looked up at Chris from below my eyelashes, trying to gauge how much he knew. "How did you know?"

"Abby, they notify the police department any time a 911 call comes in. When I heard 'Abby' and 'Blackbird Road' in the same sentence I put two and two together. You're lucky you didn't break your neck."

"I know but..."

"But nothing. I told you to stay away from that house and I meant it."

Luke shifted his feet and leaned forward, resting his elbows on his knees. "We found something in the tunnel, just before Abby fell."

Chris turned to Luke and held out his hands as if to say, *Well? Tell me.*

"There were fresh footprints in the tunnel. They were large, looked like they came from work boots or something."

"How do you know they were fresh?"

"There wasn't any dust in them. The dust hadn't settled back into the prints yet."

"And you're sure they weren't yours from the last time you were down there?"

Luke shook his head. "We didn't go down that far the last time. We didn't make it past the point where we bailed out. This time we entered through that hole and went further down so there's no way they were ours. Someone else has been down there."

Chris frowned, looking unhappy, most likely disappointed that his men had supposedly scoured that property and hadn't found anything in the way of evidence. "Well I guess that sheds a whole new light on the Hollings case. I'll have to get my men out there again. I have to go. I'm glad to see you're still alive and breathing." Chris turned and squeezed my hand, then pushed through the curtains.

"What's going on between you two?" Luke asked, looking slightly unhappy.

"Nothing. He took me out to dinner, that's all."

"He took you out to dinner? What'd he do, call you and ask you out?"

I shook my head. "Not exactly. Remember how we had to give him our names and addresses?"

"Yeah. Why?"

"Well he showed up at my house that afternoon, and then again a couple days later. That's when he asked me out to dinner."

"He showed up at your house?" Luke now looked angry. "That's not cool."

I closed my eyes and leaned back against the pillows stacked behind my head. "Luke there's nothing wrong with him wanting to take me out."

"No there's nothing wrong with it except that he showed up at your house without an invitation from you, which you hate by the way, and then did it *again*. You're involved in one of his cases. That's just not right."

"I'm not exactly involved."

"Yes you are. That house is a crime scene because of us. We brought him information about a missing child. You're part of his case. At the very least he should have waited until the case was closed and then called you like a normal person. That's just sketchy."

I started to laugh but then realized that hurt a great deal. "Don't worry about it Luke. I thought it was sweet that he liked me enough to make an excuse to come visit me. Let it go."

Shaking his head, Luke stared down at his tattered black sneakers. "Fine I'll let it go."

"Good. Now tell me why I fell because I don't quite remember what happened."

"I don't know. You got to the top of the ladder just fine and then you looked up at me, kind of sucked in your breath like you were surprised by something, and next thing I knew you disappeared."

I tried hard to think of what had surprised me but I couldn't for the life of me recall anything that happened between falling and opening my eyes in the hospital.

"Oh by the way I called your mom about a half hour ago."

"Lovely." Just as I said that I could hear my mother grilling a poor orderly out on the floor of the ER.

"Abigail Grace. What on earth did you do to yourself?" My mother swept through the curtain with her hand over her heart, pretending I was giving her heart failure with my constant presence in the emergency room. "Have they named a wing after you yet? You spend more time in the emergency room than you do anywhere else. You're too clumsy to be doing this kind of thing."

"Mom, this is the first time I've ever gotten injured exploring. And please don't make me laugh because it hurts like hell."

She came over to squeeze my hand and pulled a chair up to the side of the bed. "What happened honey? Luke said you fell?"

"Yeah I guess. I don't really remember what happened. I just know we were climbing out of a tunnel and next thing I knew I was here. Luke says something surprised me at the top of the ladder but I really can't figure out what it was."

"Well it must have been something good to knock you that far back. You know you're going to have to come stay with your dad and me for a bit until you're better. The doctor said you not only did you break your arm but you tore something in your ankle. They're going to have to fit you for one of those hideous giant boots."

"Oh come on! No! That's not cool. Dammit. Fine I'll come home with you Nurse Ratched but you know I'm going to be a terrible patient."

My mother rolled her eyes and stood, still holding onto my hand as if I might somehow fall again, perhaps right out of the hospital bed. "Don't I know it. When you were seven you had the flu the same time I did. I had to hold the bucket for you so could throw up while still holding a bucket for myself. You were miserable. You've always been miserable. It's why you're an only child."

"Very funny mom."

With a wink she pushed the curtain aside and flagged down a doctor, asking loudly when she could take her invalid daughter home. I hoped she knew I would someday get back at her for this. A few minutes later she came back in to tell me I could go home in a couple of hours after they did another set of X-rays. Luke offered to help her gather up some of my things from home as well as box up the cat for transport. It was a good thing Riley loved going in the car since he ended up at my parents' house quite frequently. Any time I got sick, injured, or had to go away for any length of time I would pack him into his crate and just drop him off. My mother would spoil him rotten for however long he was there which of course meant he never wanted to come back home with me, but he was so adaptable that he just didn't seem to care about getting shuffled around. Plus my mother really enjoyed having a cat in the house again, something she couldn't have now that my father was retired. His allergies were too severe to have a cat there full time.

After Luke left with my mother I drifted off to sleep, apparently finally feeling the effects of whatever they had given me to combat the pain I was sure to start feeling sometime in the near future. Even as a child I was a vivid dreamer, something I had yet to grow out of, but there in the hospital it was difficult to know whether I was dreaming of events as they had happened or if the drugs were causing me to see things in my sleep. Between the IV and the cast on my arm I had a hard time sleeping comfortably but I was certainly sleeping deeply, dreaming that I was back in that tunnel, putting my foot on the bottom rung of that ladder. In the dream I looked up and saw her clearly, the little girl. Had she been the surprise that had caused me to pitch backwards into the blackness? In the fog of my dream I continued to climb the ladder until I was close enough to hear sounds coming from the little girl's lips. She was saying, "You shouldn't have told him."

I was jostled awake by a nurse who was quickly disconnecting my IV, bumping into the side of my bed and yanking a bit harder on things than she needed. I winced and drew in a sharp breath as she yanked the IV needle out of the back of my hand but she didn't even bat an eye. Apparently she had done what she was asked to do and she left without a word, leaving me to assume I was either going home or being prepped for embalming. Either outcome was fine with me as long as someone could stop the throbbing in the back of my hand. I closed my eyes again, trying to block out the harsh fluorescent lights, and waited for someone to come tell me what was going on. My arm was starting to ache, as was my ankle, which reminded me that my mother had said something about one of those horrible walking casts. Finally a man in a white coat parted the bile colored curtains and smiled at me.

"Hi Abigail, I'm Doctor Franklin. So you'll be ready to be discharged just as soon as you get fitted for a cast on that ankle. Here's your discharge summary, a prescription for some pain killers, and a prescription for some anti-inflammatories that you'll want to take pretty regularly to keep the swelling down. Any questions?"

I shook my head. "No I think I'm all set. How long do I have to stay in the cast? And the boot for that matter?"

"The cast will need to be checked in a few weeks. You can do that at your primary care. The boot will be more involved. I'm going to set you up with a podiatrist in a few days to make sure that tendon tear doesn't need surgery."

"Argh..." I groaned and covered my face with my hand. "Just my luck."

The doctor chuckled as he signed the discharge papers. "My nurse should be down in a few minutes to get you in that boot. Your mother is coming back to get you momentarily. Which means I'm going to go hide."

"Good idea. Sorry about her. She can be a bit..."

"Yes, I got that memo," he said, glancing furtively over his shoulder to make sure my mother wasn't lurking somewhere in the ER. "Good luck Abigail."

"Thanks Doctor Franklin."

He left and moments later a petite blond nurse was fitting me with this ugly, clunky black boot that made me look like the bionic woman. "Now make sure it's tight enough to lend support but not so tight that you can't feel your toes."

"Do I have to wear this to bed too?"

"Yes you do, sorry to say. But since they're not sure how bad the tear is just yet you have to wear it at all times to keep that foot stable. The only time you should be taking it off is when you need to shower. And my advice is that you shower sitting down and make sure there's someone there to give you a hand so you don't slip."

I looked down at her perfectly coiffed hair and wondered if slapping her would make her a bit less cheerful while delivering bad news to patients but reminded myself it wasn't her fault that I had dumped myself off of a ladder. It's not like it was the first time I had done something like that. Nor was it likely to be the last.

"Now let's get you to swing your legs over the side of the bed and see if you can put some weight on that boot."

Thankfully they had dressed me in blue scrub pants at some point so swinging my legs over the side of the bed was not nearly as embarrassing as it could have been. I couldn't believe how heavy that thing was. It was like have a 40-pound cement block strapped to my ankle. This was going to be a fun recuperation.

"Ok see if you can put some pressure on that foot and stand up. It's going to feel strange."

That was an understatement. It felt like I had someone else's foot attached to my leg. I stood and wobbled a bit, hoping I would fall down and break yet another bone in my body. Thankfully I managed to stay upright but it hurt like hell to have my body weight on that foot. My mother came back in the room just as I flopped back onto the bed.

"Stay off it as much as possible," the nurse warned. "Someone will give you a call about the appointment with the podiatrist. And you should call your primary care as soon as you get home."

"Come on gimpy." My mother grabbed my arm and helped me up as I hobbled out to her car. It was exhausting just to lower myself into my mother's Impala and put on my seatbelt. She drove at a breakneck speed, explaining to me that the faster she drove the less painful all the bumps would be. Somehow I wasn't sure that logic was exactly sound.

"Mom, can we just get to the house in one piece?"

My parents' house hadn't changed much since my childhood. They had bought it when I was only eight months old and, strangely enough, it had been abandoned when they decided it would be the perfect fixer upper. My father always said the plan was to fix it up and get out after ten years but thirty plus years later they were still in the house, still constantly fixing it up which drove my mother insane. The house was a small green and white cape on a corner lot, which had doubled in size when my mother shrewdly snapped up the lot next door when I was about twelve years old. She kept the town from allowing a four-plex to be built there and instead had created a backyard oasis of irises, climbing roses, and a pond surrounded by butterfly bushes and cone flowers. It was my favorite thing about the house.

Since I had moved out my mother hadn't done much to change my bedroom. It was a lot less cluttered of course since it was difficult for anyone over the age of twenty to squeeze their entire life into one room but otherwise it looked remarkably the same as it always had. My white wrought iron twin bed was pushed in the corner next to the closet door with the bureau in the other corner. A mission style desk sat under the bank of three windows that overlooked the backyard with a solid wood captain's chair tucked under it. The desk's surface was clear now, my computer no longer there, and the piles of books I had amassed no longer crowded the floors but it always felt like home when I was there.

Riley was already waiting for me in the front hallway, obviously having settled himself in just as he usually did. My camera bag, backpack, and writing bag were all sitting on the floor waiting to be carried upstairs. It looked like between Luke and my mom they had managed to grab most everything that I could want. I bent and opened up my backpack to see that it was crammed with the four novels and two mental health books that had been sitting on my bedside table along with the notebook I always kept when I was reading in case I wanted to take notes or write down quotes I liked.

My writing bag seemed to have each of my favorite pens along with a bag of mechanical pencils and all of the notes I had been taking for my new story. "Boy you two sure know how to pack for a girl."

"Do you want tea Abby?"

"Does a bear...well you know. Yes I'd love tea."

I tottered into the kitchen and lowered myself into a kitchen chair where Riley immediately hauled himself into my lap.

"So tell me again what you two were doing at that house?"

"The usual. We explored it a couple of weeks ago and found out it had tunnels. I guess it was a stop on the Underground Railroad. We decided to go back and check out the tunnels to see how far they went but while we were down there we found footprints. Fresh ones."

"And? So you weren't the only ones exploring down there. That's not unusual."

"It wouldn't be under normal circumstances but there's a little girl missing from that neighborhood. In that case fresh footprints become evidence."

"I think that's stretching it a bit but I see why you might come to that conclusion." My mother sat down across from me and placed a mug of tea in front of me along with a pile of animal crackers. She knew me so well. Then she slid painkiller towards me. "Take that. The one's they gave you in the hospital are most likely about to wear off."

"They certainly are. It feels like there's an elephant sitting on my arm."

"Well, there is," she said, gesturing towards Riley who had somehow managed to wrap himself around my casted arm and was purring contentedly. Bizarre little animal.

Just as I swallowed the painkiller with a gulp of tea there was a knock at the door. My mother stood and headed for the front door and when she opened it, I could see Detective Benson standing on the porch.

"Mrs. Brandt. I'm Detective Chris Benson."

"Nice to meet you Detective. What did my daughter do now?"

"Mom!" I tried to stand up but I had moved too quickly and ended up tipping backwards and missing the kitchen chair, landing on the linoleum floor with a thud. "Well, that wasn't embarrassing at all."

Chris had followed my mother into the kitchen and reached around her to help me back up and into the chair. "She didn't do anything," he said, trying not to laugh. "I was just coming by to see how she was doing."

"I'm fine. In fact I was considering going dancing a little later." I shot out, pitching the sarcasm out of my mouth before I could think better of it.

"Whoa there cripple, let's be a little nicer to the law." My mother couldn't help but smirk in my direction knowing that my biting wit was all her fault. She turned to Chris and put a conciliatory hand on his arm. "You have to forgive my daughter. She's on drugs."

"Mom! I am not on drugs!"

"Well technically you are dear. Lots of them. In fact you just took some, remember?" She looked from Chris, to me, then back to Chris, gauging his reaction to her teasing. "That's why she fell down. She falls down a lot when she's taking pills."

I put my head in my hands and groaned. "Argh. Why couldn't I have been an orphan?"

Having had her fun, my mother headed for the pantry and began pulling mugs off of a shelf. "Would everyone like tea? Yes? Good. Coming right up."

I loved how she never waited for anyone to answer her. With my good foot I pushed a chair out for Chris to sit in while my mother bustled around the kitchen putting on more tea. Come to think of it though, I was beginning to feel just a wee bit woozy...

"So, how are you feeling?" Chris asked, reaching out and covering my hand with his.

"I feel very much like I got run over." I leaned forward and rested my cheek on the table as the room began to spin. Boy those pain killers worked fast. "I think I might need to go lay down."

Chris laughed and patted me on the head, then stood to leave. "I think I'll head out and let you rest. Try not to get hurt any worse than you already are."

I could feel the medicine pulling my eyelids shut, my mouth with it, so I was unable to do much more than grunt my goodbyes to Chris before almost completely passing out at the kitchen table.

My mother walked Chris to the door, then came back to help me to bed. She guided me up the stairs and into my twin bed, tucking the blankets around me and kissing me on the forehead. It was good to be home.

Chapter 14

The next morning my mother woke me with a cup of tea and more painkillers. It had been an uncomfortable sleep since I couldn't really roll over and I am a definite stomach sleeper. Sleeping flat on my back was generally tortuous for me. I spent most of the morning propped up in bed reading. My mother had picked up a copy of Rachel Florence's book "The Bloodline" for me and by lunch I was already halfway through it. It was the story of an aristocrat who murdered her child and was subsequently committed to an asylum. My mother always knew how best to take care of me. The key to speedy recovery is always a good book.

I looked down at both my casts and sighed. Sometimes I wondered if my parents had some sort of window into my future when they chose Grace as my middle name. My clumsiness was legendary amongst my friends and family but this stunt certainly took the cake. It was the first time in 30 years I had needed a cast and I certainly wish I could have continued to go without.

Sitting up, I reached to the foot of my bed where my mother had conveniently left my father's laptop. I pulled up the Internet and searched for news on the Hollings' missing girl but it seemed as if there hadn't been any movement at all, nothing that might give that poor family some hope that their child was still alive. I pulled some papers out of my writing bag and found the property deeds from the farmhouse. I shuffled through them again, reading the article about the fire for a second time, letting my mind wander. I imagined the scene that erupted in those woods as townspeople searched fervently for evidence of tunnels and of slaves. The entrance Luke and I had found in the basement must have been well hidden, as the exit must have been as well, wherever that might be. It was the perfect place for a murderer to escape to. I fell back asleep dreaming of that fire, my drug addled brain conjuring a black and shadowy form running through the tunnels holding a wispy, glowing white girl in its arms. I tried desperately to see his face but my dream wouldn't allow me to. I could see the little girl's face though, and it was a face I had seen before.

****

My recovery was slow and aggravating. There were only so many books a girl could read before going a bit stir crazy. It was an unseasonably mild day in the middle of the week so I grabbed a new novel, Jack Treby's "The Scandal at Bletchley", and slid down the stairs on my rear so I could sit out on the porch to read. It was a much-needed change in scenery.

The screen door opened and Riley came charging out onto the porch, my mother close behind with a cup of tea in one hand and my pain pills in the other. "You starting to ache yet there dear?"

I nodded, suddenly feeling a dull pain in my arm that was quickly climbing the charts. She handed me a pill and the tea, then sat in the wicker chair opposite me, leaning back to look through the screens and out to the yard. The porch was my mother's second favorite thing about the house. My parents had bought it abandoned nearly 30 years ago, when I was just a little tyke. Having a screened-in porch had allowed for many comfortable evenings sitting out watching thunderstorms or looking at the stars. Sometimes we could even hear music drifting over from the concerts that played every fall at the fair grounds in the center of town. In all it was a pretty idyllic spot. That house had inspired my imagination for years. I first read "Anne of Green Gables" under my bed with a flashlight in my hand. I wrote my first story in that house after my parents took me to see an abandoned lakeside restaurant. I was entranced by the Starlight Lounge, so empty and forlorn on the shores of a graying lake, and I promptly sat down and wrote my first ghost story. It was a great house.

"So, tell me about this detective. I'm guessing his visit today had to do with a bit more than just checking up on a witness in his case."

I smiled at my mother's ability to ferret out any and all information about my personal life. "I went to dinner with him. Once."

"So I gather from Luke that you two had something to do with a case?"

"Yeah," I nodded, taking a sip of my tea to chase away the fuzzy feeling creeping into my brain. "Luke and I went to explore a little cottage out in Athol which normally wouldn't have been an issue but I found a box tucked under a bed. It was souvenirs from a number of unsolved cases back in the day. Kidnappings. Murders. Little girls. At the same time a little girl in the same neighborhood went missing and we were worried the box had some connection. We brought it to the police station and it turned out that Chris was in charge of the case. He stopped by my apartment and asked me to dinner."

My mother's brow creased and she looked suddenly thoughtful. "He came to your apartment?"

"Yeah, why?"

"How did he get your address?"

"From the police report I would assume."

"And you didn't find that odd that he chose to just turn up at your house?" she asked, her voice taking on an edge of concern. "Didn't he also have your phone number on that report?"

I thought about it for a moment. "I suppose he did."

"Abby, far be it for me to get involved, but that just sounds strange to me."

"Mom, it's no big deal. In fact it was kind of cute. He asked all about my photography and everything."

My mother sighed and made the face that usually meant she was giving in even though she still didn't agree with me and probably never would. "Ok, but be careful. You don't really know anything about this guy."

"I know mom. But he's a cop. He seems like a nice guy."

"I'll trust you on that. You usually have pretty good instincts but I still want you to watch it."

"Yeah yeah. I will. But right now I need to sleep off these pills. You have to stop feeding them to me like they're Pez."

She laughed and stood, taking the teacup from me. "Come on grandma, I'll help you up to bed."

Chapter 15

Detective Chris Benson pulled his unmarked car onto the lawn of the old Murray farm and got out, looking up at the house. He was disgusted with himself for not getting back there earlier but he had gotten lucky when Abby fell from that ladder. It saved him from having to figure out how to get her out of the way himself. Following the path around the side of the house, the detective stepped easily over the barbed wire and found the hole that Luke and Abby had used to get into the tunnel. Chris pulled out a flashlight and peered down into the tunnel below, the ladder still propped where the pair had left it after getting Abby out and into an ambulance. He swung a leg onto the ladder, then anchored both feet on the top rung. He stuck his flashlight between his teeth and climbed down into the darkness, turning quickly and heading in the direction of the woods.

Of course he felt terrible that Abby was hurt. He liked her, liked talking to her, and had enjoyed their dinner date, but he also had a job to do. In this case his job was to make sure no one else saw those footprints. As he walked he wondered what he would have done if Abby hadn't gotten hurt. He would have needed a way to keep her quiet about what she had seen in the tunnel, and her friend too. Shaking his head, Chris tried not to think about it, hoping he could convince the two of them that they hadn't seen anything important down there. In the meantime he came upon the footprints and pulled a handkerchief out of his pocket. No one carried handkerchiefs anymore, he thought, but everyone underestimated the many uses for handkerchiefs. Kneeling down, he used the handkerchief to dust away all the evidence that his brother had been down here. Again.

Chapter 16

He watched from the woods as his little brother climbed down into the tunnel. He didn't understand why Chris was so hell bent on saving his ass but there he was, covering his tracks for him yet again. Sometimes he wondered why Chris didn't just tell the world that his brother was a miscreant. All it would take was one well-placed call to his wife and Chris could blow his brother's cover, but instead Chris just tried his best to keep the elder Benson from getting caught, the same way he used to cover for their father whenever he came home drunk and dirty, using the same cut through in the woods.

He kept his eyes on the Murray farm until he could see Chris's head pop from the hole in the lawn. He waited until he heard the door of Chris's unmarked car slam shut before turning and heading home. After all, dinner would be waiting for him and now, thanks to his brother, he could enjoy it without worry.

Chapter 17

Cabin fever overtook me around the second week at my mother's. As much as I enjoyed her company, I enjoyed my freedom far more. I also enjoyed being able to get around on my own but I was still two more weeks away from that goal. I had gone to see the doctor for both my arm and my ankle. Thankfully he was rather optimistic about my prognosis though the only words I really heard as he was talking were, "two more weeks in the cast and the boot". The fact that I hadn't done any permanent damage to my limbs was completely lost on me as I wallowed in self-pity, whining about how itchy my cast was and how tired I was of clumping around in my boot.

"I need to get out of this house. I need to do something other than sit and read!"

My mother laughed, loud and hard. "I never thought I'd hear you of all people say that. I would think you'd be able to sit and read forever."

"Nope. I've had it. I'm going for a walk."

I hobbled down the front steps and out into the street, feeling drained from just that little bit of effort. There was no way I was going to make it any farther than that so I turned around and went to sit on the front stoop feeling defeated. As I sat and wallowed I heard a car pull up and Luke hopped out with a stack of art supplies in his hand. "Yo. You up for a bit of art therapy my friend?"

I nodded vigorously, happy to be given an alternative to reading or writing, which I couldn't do with my arm in a cast anyway. It was pretty difficult to type with only one hand. Thankfully it was my left arm that was in a cast so I could still paint with Luke. He spread huge sheets of canvas out on the sidewalk and pulled a few spray cans out of a box.

"So how's the arm and whatnot?" Luke shook a can of black paint and started outlining the letter "A" on a piece of canvas. I clumsily picked out a can of pink paint and started spraying unidentifiable blotches onto another canvas.

"Hurts like hell. It also itches."

Luke continued to spray the outline of my entire name, then capped the black paint. "Don't use a pencil to scratch it. There are all kinds of urban legends about using a pencil to scratch under your cast. None of them end well." He had picked up a can of turquoise and began filling in the letters with streaks and bubbles.

"I hadn't planned on it. So did you get a chance to tell Chris...I mean Detective Benson about the footprints?"

"Yeah I did," he said, using a can of yellow paint to add arrows and sunbursts to the canvas. "He looked pretty upset about it. Like way more upset than he should have been."

"What do you mean?"

"I mean he looked pissed. Like the footprints were a problem rather than evidence."
"That's odd. He didn't say anything to me when he was here."

Luke looked up from his painting and scowled at me. "He was here?"

"Yeah. He came to check on me after I got out of the hospital."

"How did he know where to find you?" he asked, putting the spray can down.

"I don't know. I figured he asked someone at the hospital."

"Abby, don't you find it somewhat odd that this guy just keeps showing up where you are? Does he not know how to use a phone?"

"Not you too..." I muttered.

"What'd you say?"

"I said, what's wrong with him checking up on me?"

Luke sighed and reached for another paint can. "It's just weird Abbs. Normal people ask for a phone number and call you before randomly showing up where you are. Especially when you're not even at your own house. That just strikes me as totally inappropriate."

"He's a cop Luke. And he's a nice guy. Just drop it."

"Fine." Luke turned back to his painting, dropping the subject, not saying much at all after that. He rarely got angry but in this case I could tell he was upset. What on earth did he and my mother think Chris was up to? He liked me. What was so wrong with that?

We sat in virtual silence for another half hour, until my mother realized Luke was outside with me. "Luke! How are you? There's a furry little boy inside who would love to see you!"

"Hey Mrs. Brandt. Yeah I guess I could come in and say hi to Riley." He stood without even looking at me and went inside with my mother, leaving me to struggle to get up on my own. I had never seen him like this. I tottered inside and lowered myself onto the couch. Luke sat on the floor petting Riley who was in pig heaven, so in love was he with Luke. My mother sat in the easy chair with another cup of tea and chattered at Luke. He still wouldn't look at me.

After he had left my mother sat down next to me on the couch and put her arm around me. "What's going on between you and Luke?"

"Nothing really." I sighed. "He said the same thing you did about Chris. That it's weird that he just shows up."

"Well honey, it is weird. But give him the benefit of the doubt that he has good intentions, just make sure you keep an open mind and watch yourself. You usually have pretty good instincts."

"Thanks mom. I will." I rolled my eyes at the level of overprotectiveness going on but I suppose it was somewhat warranted. When it came to men I generally allowed my good judgment to take some time off, ignoring red flags more often than not. I had had a string of less than pleasant relationships, many of which my mother ended up having to help me clean up after so her concern was certainly understandable.

I sat miserably at the kitchen table while my mother started pulling out ingredients for dinner. I was staring dumbly into space when the front page of the newspaper, which was lying on the fourth, unused chair to my right, caught my eye. The headline read, "SEARCH FOR MISSING GIRL ABANDONED". There were no leads, no evidence had been discovered and so the police had called off the search. It had been too long, said a spokesperson for the department. They could no longer justify the resources and man-hours that were being allocated for the search. Anyone with further information was encouraged to contact Detective Chris Benson.

So that was it. The police were assuming that Nicole Hollings was dead. Obviously the footprint in the tunnel had meant nothing then. It was probably left behind by one of the officers who checked the tunnel and we had just jumped to conclusions. It was so sad to think of that poor little girl out there somewhere.

I stood and headed for the living room couch, my head feeling heavy with both exhaustion and sadness. The moment I laid down I fell asleep and began to dream. Almost immediately the little girl from the photo appeared in my dream. She was standing in the backyard of Green Gables, staring off into the woods. A breeze stumbled through the trees, rocking their branches back and forth but the girl was still. Her dress didn't move, her hair lay flat down her back in neat little ringlets. It was as if she was completely unaffected by her surroundings. Her little hands were clenched tight at her sides and her body fairly vibrated. I willed my dream to carry me over to her so I could see her face and I was suddenly transported into the dream, standing right in front of her and watching her jaw flex, her face creased with anger.

She tilted her head, still looking past me into the woods, and sighed. "She's still alive."

***

I woke with a start, shivering with cold, my heart pumping in my chest. The child's breathy, ethereal voice echoed repeatedly in my head. *She's still alive.* It could likely have been wishful thinking that had conjured up such a dream but it had felt so real, as if I was truly standing in front of her, listening to her speak, feeling her breath on my face. I could even feel the breeze that seemed not to disturb her yet it raised gooseflesh on my own arms. Why had she been looking out toward the woods? Was there something out there that the investigators had missed? That wasn't possible, I thought. They had combed that entire area. I remembered reading in the paper that they had gridded off the woods and sent in teams with dogs. If Nicole Hollings had been in those woods the police would have found her.

Then I wondered if perhaps the woods held a clue as to who had taken her. Perhaps the girl in my dream was staring out at some evidence that would point to the kidnapper. Then again it was only a dream with no basis in reality. I was not about to admit to Chris that I had once seen a spirit who had pointed me in the direction of a murderer and now I was seeing another. He would likely have me committed! I grabbed the remote control and turned on the TV hoping that the noise would help clear my head. I needed to lose myself in someone else's unreality for a while.

No matter how I tried to focus on the television I still could not shake the remnants of my dream. I continued to stare at the screen, watching the plot of some terrible daytime drama unfold in front of me, when I heard my the screen door slam and my father's key in the door. I looked down at the clock on the cable box and realized it was already 4:30 and almost time for dinner.

"Hey kiddo." My father slipped off his shoes and jammed his feet in his slippers, then dropped his keys on the antique icebox in the kitchen.

"Hey dad. How did your doctor's appointment go?" A few months ago he had had surgery on his elbow but his hand still wasn't regaining much feeling or flexibility, something that worried him daily until he finally scheduled an appointment to see his neurosurgeon.

"Eh, he said it's going to take time. I guess I did a lot more damage to it than usual and it's going to be a while before it's back to something resembling normal." He was yelling to me from the kitchen, which I knew drove my mother nuts so I hoisted myself off the couch and hobbled in to sit with him. He was in the middle of pouring himself a gin and tonic. "Want one?"

"On top of pain killers? No way." I said, chuckling.

He turned and looked at me over his shoulder as he squirted lime into his foggy drink. "You sure? It might be fun."

"Dad! You're not supposed to drink when you're taking narcotics."

He reached into his pocket and drew out what I assumed was a bottle of his own painkillers from his earlier visit to the surgeon. He peered at the label, tapping a little red sticker with his index finger. "Well I'll be damned. You're right." He stuck the bottle back in his pocket and continued to pour his drink. "Oh well. One drink won't kill either one of us."

And so I sat at the table and drank with my father. He asked me about work and about my photography. I told him I was looking forward to September and the new school year since I would have a new group of students. He asked about my writing but of course I had very little to report on that front. I seemed to have completely run out of inspiration and ideas, my ability to put a solid thought on paper almost nonexistent. My dad listened while sipping his drink, occasionally asking more questions or tossing out a comment here and there.

"So how's the leg feeling?"

I shrugged. "It's still there. Still hurts. Hurts a little less though. I haven't been taking nearly as many painkillers, although mom keeps trying to feed them to me like they're M&Ms."

"Sounds about right." He chuckled, fishing the ice out of the bottom of his glass. He caught me looking at him and grinned. "Leave no gin behind."

We sat and chatted until my mother came down to start dinner, which I would have loved to help with since I enjoyed cooking, but of course that wasn't going to happen with my arm in a cast.

It was closer to three weeks before the cast came off my arm. The day the doctor took a saw to the plaster was the happiest day of my life. The boot came off the same day and the doctor fitted me for a custom insole for my shoes, warning me not to wear flip flops or flats for a while. When I finally stood and put both feet on the floor I was surprised at just how much strength I had lost. I moved slowly out to the car where my mother was waiting, feeling like someone else's foot was attached to my leg.

"Well Peg Leg, how does it feel to have the boot off?"

"It feels strange," I said, lowering myself into the car. "And itchy. My skin is all dry from being in that thing for so long."

My mother leaned over and looked at my arm. "Your arm looks like a chicken leg."

"Thanks mom." Looking down at my arm I could see that she was right. It was skinny and scaly, my fingers stiff and achy. "At least I can move it freely now."

"Just don't overdo it," she said, steering her Impala in the direction of home. "It's going to be a little while before it's back up to strength."

"I know. I'll be careful with it. I don't feel like having to get it recast."
We made it to the house where I was surprised to see Luke waiting for me. My mother must have called him because I hadn't talked to him since the day he went off on me about Detective Benson.

"Hey Abbs. Your mom told me it was celebration time." He reached out and handed me a bottle of red wine, a nice Pinot Noir that had probably cost him a bit more than it should have.

"Thanks man. Come on. Let's go sit. My foot is killing me."

Laughing, we went inside and cracked open the wine, then settled down on the couch. "So have there been any breaks in the kidnapping?"

I shook my head. "Detective Benson said they've called off the search. They're going on the assumption that the girl is dead. Which is sad, but probably pretty accurate. They say the chances of a kidnapping victim being found alive any time after 48 hours have passed is slim. She's been gone for weeks now."

"You're right, that is sad." Luke sighed and leaned back on the couch. "I'm glad you're on the mend though. We don't have much longer before the end of summer and then I'm going to be on a plane to Oregon."

"I know. I can't imagine you being that far away. I'm going to have exploring withdrawals."

Luke chuckled. "You'll be fine. I'm sure you'll find someone else to explore with. Like maybe that Dave kid we met a few weeks ago. Remember? The one we ran into at the state school?"

"Oh yeah! The kid with the really white teeth." That was the single most memorable thing about Dave. His teeth were blindingly white and perfectly straight. He looked like he stepped out of an Abercrombie catalog; the polar opposite of Luke who occasionally looked like he was on his way to rob a Seven Eleven.

"It's going to be a long year," he admitted. "But I'll be back next summer."

Next summer was months away but I was trying not to think about. Luke had become such a constant, reassuring presence in my life. We spent almost every weekend together and it would be strange not being able to call him up and have him meet me somewhere to explore. It was going to be a long year.

Chapter 18

The Murray Farm sat in shadow, the summer heat drifting around its white clapboard siding. The day itself was sunny and hazy, but the overgrown trees kept the house cool and dark. Michael Benson, slightly taller and thinner than his younger brother, sat in the living room of the little cottage, staring at the books stacked haphazardly on the shelves. So many people had come through the house over the years, touching things and moving things. It had only been a matter of time before someone found that box upstairs just like he had when he was young. He used to break in there when he was young even though there were still people living there. He would wait until the occupants were asleep and sneak upstairs to the small bedroom in the back. Once when he was about seven years old he had heard his mother saying that the room used to belong to a little girl who lived there, but she had been murdered.

Back then Michael hadn't known what murder was all about. He had no concept of death or violence, but once it had been explained to him he found that he was fascinated by the whole idea of taking someone's life away from them. Then he found the box. It was full of lives that had been taken by someone, a man who had never been identified, let alone caught and punished for his crimes. That was the first time he could remember wondering if he too could get away with taking a life.

He started small, like other sociopaths, torturing animals and harassing the smaller children in the neighborhood. He got an unexplainable thrill watching those who were weaker than he have their spirits crushed. It was an incredible rush of control and power that he knew, even at a young age, would become addictive.

Though his desire to take lives would grow through the years, he became skilled at hiding that part of himself from the rest of the world. He managed to finish school, graduate from college, and eventually get married. He even had children of his own, and though he particularly enjoyed preying on children, he justified it carefully by telling himself he would never do any harm to his own. Nor would he ever harm his wife. His own family was sacred.

That was why, when his brother found out what Michael truly was, he didn't hurt him or try to force his silence. He simply trusted that his little brother would protect his blood, and he was right. Chris had taken Michael's secret into his heart and kept it there, expertly covering for Michael on the rare instances when the evil inside him crept out at the wrong times.

There was one incident with another child in their neighborhood who was a favorite target of Michael's. The child had wandered away from the other children on the playground and Michael was waiting. He grabbed the little boy by the hair with one hand while wrapping the long, strong fingers of his other hand around the child's throat, watching the little one's eyes bulge with fear. The fear was always Michael's favorite part. It was what spurred him on and pushed him to experiment with the many ways he could inflict it on another human being. Unfortunately that day the little boy's fear turned to fight and he lashed out at Michael, reaching out and scratching Michael's face. The older boy roared in anger, his face purple with rage and hatred. He struck the boy as hard as he could, knocking him to the ground, but his own shout had attracted the attention of the adults who were monitoring their children on the playground. One of the mothers began to walk towards the two boys, Michael standing over the little boy, seething.

As the mother approached, her faced etched with worry and concern, Chris was coming through the woods, searching for his brother. He had learned early on that Michael should never be left alone because there was no telling what he would get up to. In fact Chris would see his mother shake her head in defeat, telling their father that she couldn't do a thing with that boy, so he had taken it upon himself to keep an eye on Michael even though he was three full years younger. He found that he wasn't afraid of Michael even though everyone else seemed to be. He knew that other parents didn't let their children come over the

Benson house because of Michael. They said there was something very wrong with him. And they were right, though they could never find proof to back up their suspicions. That was because of Chris. Rushing through the trees, Chris could see that something was wrong as his brother stood over the little boy who had stopped moving near Michael's feet. His brother's anger was still evident on his face and Chris could see Michael drawing back his foot to deliver a kick that would most certainly kill the boy. That is if he wasn't already dead.

Chris closed the distance between himself and his brother, grabbing Michael by the arm to snap him out of his trance. "Michael don't. That mother will see you and that will be it. You'll go to jail for sure."

Michael was breathing hard, staring at the mother who was approaching. Chris stepped in front of him and grabbed him by both shoulders, shaking him until he finally focused on his little brother's face. "You need to calm down. We're going to pretend to be helping the little boy and when that lady gets over here, I'm going to tell her that he fell and hit his head on a rock. Michael, do you understand what I'm saying?"

Michael nodded, lowering his foot back to the ground. He tried his best to arrange his face into an expression that conveyed concern even though he still wanted to reach down and snap the child's neck for scratching him. Chris was right though. It would be a waste for him to go to jail now that he had discovered just how intoxicating it could be to inflict pain on another human being.

Chris played it off perfectly, explaining to the woman that he and Michael had been playing in the woods and had seen the little boy running towards them. He told her in earnest tones that the boy had tripped over something and hit his head on a rock, but that he and Michael had been too far away to do anything about it. The woman looked from Chris to Michael and back again, but it seemed that she believed Chris when he said that Michael's face had gotten scratched by some low hanging branches when he was running to check on the boy.

Michael helped the woman scoop up the unconscious boy and the brothers watched as she carted him back to the rest of the mothers who squealed with shock and worry. That was the first time Chris had intervened like that and he had done it beautifully.

Now, as adults, Chris had taken on an even more active role in protecting his brother. He had joined the police force with the idea that someday his murderous brother would slip up, and when that happened (not if, but when) Chris knew Michael would need someone on his side. Someone who had some weight to throw around. So far Chris had not had to actively intervene between his brother and the law, but he knew it was only a matter of time before that would be the case.

Once Chris made detective Michael knew he was protected. He also knew he now had the freedom to use the box. That box had become an obsession for him and once the cottage was abandoned he would spend hours alone in that upstairs bedroom, poring over the articles and the locks of hair. He even began stockpiling weapons in the house, hiding them in closets and in the bureau drawers underneath the moldy clothing. He knew he was getting obsessed, addicted to the information in that box, but he had decided it was his turn. He wanted to fill his own box.

Michael waited, and planned, and imagined until that sunny afternoon when he was on his way home from the cottage. He always cut through the woods so that he could tell his wife he was out walking, taking in nature, even though she rarely asked where he had been. She trusted him for some strange reason, which amused him greatly because if she knew what her husband was truly capable of she would take the children and run. But since she had no idea what Michael hid inside himself, she simply lived her life the way other wives and mothers did, without fear. That afternoon was different though. He was walking through the woods when he caught sight of a flash of color in the trees and heard the pounding of feet. The steps slowed down and he heard the whisper of a little girl's voice singing some kind of rhyme. He quickened his pace, moving closer until he could see that it was the Hollings girl that lived over on Blackbird Road.

At that moment I had no idea what took him over but something drove him to follow the girl through the woods until he saw her break through the trees, heading for the Caron place. He watched as she bounded up the stairs and knocked on the back door of the little yellow house. The screen door opened and she disappeared inside, and even though Michael could no longer see her he didn't move from his spot behind a pine tree. A few minutes later the Hollings girl bounded outside with the Caron girl and ran for the swing set in their backyard. He watched the two girls play for what seemed like hours; until it began to get dark and the Hollings girl shouted something about having to get home.

Michael watched her come back out through the screen door and head for the trees, completely oblivious to the fact that she was being watched. Stalked, like prey. It wasn't a conscious decision to take her. Something inside Michael decided on its own that she would be the perfect first addition to his own box— especially that shiny blond hair of hers. It would look perfect wound up in a loop with a piece of ribbon.

Chapter 19

Chris Benson stood at the tiny, grimy window of the squad room with a cup of tea in his hand, wondering how Abby was doing. He hated being in this kind of position. After all, he really liked Abby and enjoyed spending time with her, but he also had a duty to protect his brother. Sometimes he wished his brother could just be normal so that Chris could have the life he wanted. He wanted to get married, have a few kids, and find a new job. He had never had any desire to be a cop; he had only done it because of Michael. Now he was tired of solving other people's crimes simply on the off chance that someday he would need to help Michael out of a jam. Like he was doing now.

The day the Hollings girl was reported missing Chris had a bad feeling. In fact he had had a bad feeling since the day Michael and his wife had moved back into that neighborhood. Even before Abby had brought him that box he had known about the murders at the Murray Farm. His brother had been the first one to bring him that box when they were kids and living in that exact same neighborhood, just two houses down from where Michael and his wife lived now. Chris knew the moment Michael moved his family into the new house that his brother had an ulterior motive. He wanted to be close to that house.

The first time Michael had shown him the box Chris had been horrified. He couldn't understand how a human being could take the lives of so many innocent children, but his brother was fascinated. It was sickening. At first Chris tried to ignore his brother's constant mention of the box's contents, his excitement about the fact that the murderer had never been caught. But as they grew older and Chris was forced to intervene more and more often as his brother became more and more violent, he realized that the box was a problem. He also realized that one day Michael would attempt to recreate the events contained in that box.

And now he had. He had taken the Hollings girl and hidden her somewhere in the tunnels under the Murray Farm. Chris honestly had no idea how far those tunnels went but he knew the girl was down there, and he knew the girl was dead. It took every ounce of strength he had to convince the department to drop the search for her. Then he had had one of his subordinates notify the parents that the search had been called off and their daughter assumed dead.

He hated himself for what he had done. In fact, as he stood staring out the window, he decided it was time for him to hand in his resignation. But first he had to find a way to stop his brother, once and for all.

Chapter 20

I was surprised that I hadn't heard from Chris in a few weeks. I was excited to have the cast and the boot off and was hoping to find my way out of my house but it seemed that no one was around. Luke was off finishing up his preparations for grad school—packing, spending time with his girlfriend—and Chris was strangely incommunicado.

I shrugged to myself as I made my first cup of tea back in my own apartment. It was a relief to be back in my own home, as much as I loved spending time with my parents. I moved slowly, putting away all the books and writing materials I had collected at my parents' house over the past few months. My office was a bit of a disaster but it was wonderful to be back in my own domain.

As I lowered myself onto the reading bench under the hall window my cell phone rang. I looked quickly at the caller ID to see that it was Luke. "Hey. Are you done packing yet?"

"Not yet. But I was going through my camera gear and realized that the folder I keep my memory cards in is missing."

"Oh, that's not good. When was the last time you had it?"

"Honestly I haven't touched my gear since the day you fell. I haven't even looked at the shots I took that day."

I could hear him rummaging around, probably still sorting through all his belongings. Being a number of years younger than I, Luke had graduated from college only a year before and had been sharing an apartment with a friend, an arrangement he would be leaving behind in order to go to Oregon for graduate school. That meant he had to pack every last thing he owned as he wouldn't be going back. During the summer he would be staying with his parents if and when he managed to come back to the east coast.

"Any chance you could go out there and see if it's laying around anywhere?"

My mouth sagged open and I stuttered a bit as I considered what Luke had just asked me. "You want me to go back to the house?"

"Just the yard Abbs. I have to assume it fell out when I reached into my bag to call the ambulance. That was the last time I remember seeing it."

"Can't you do it?"

"No. I'm in the middle of packing. It would take me almost a half hour to get out to the house. Lara is on her way over to help me load the last few boxes into the car."

I sighed. "I still don't understand why you're driving out there. Why don't you just ship your stuff and take a plane?"

"Because it's too expensive. My last paycheck went to rent and textbooks. Plus Lara wants to be able to come with me. She's going to drive out there, stay for a few days, and then fly back on her own."

"Fine," I said, knowing that Luke probably struggled with the idea of asking me to go back to the house. "I'll go see if it's there. I'll call you in a bit."
I climbed into my car and slowly made my way to the house. By the time I pulled into the layby on the side of Blackbird Road my foot was sore from pressing down on the gas pedal. I unfolded

myself from the car and rolled my ankle left and right to stretch it out a bit before putting my weight on it. Standing, I stretched quickly and started walking toward the house in a slow, painful trudging manner that took forever. I stopped for a moment in the front yard to catch my breath. It disappointed me when I realized that the house was no longer intriguing. Now it seemed almost frightening. I turned the corner into the backyard and climbed carefully over the barbed wire, which was difficult as it hurt quite a bit to put my full body weight on my right foot.

Taking it slowly I combed the backyard but the grass had grown much higher than it was the last time Luke and I had been there. I would have thought a black leather memory card folder would stick out but I was wrong. I had to bend at the waist and move the grass aside with my right food. The closer I got to the hole in the grass that led to the tunnel, the less hope I had that I would find Luke's memory cards and the more I feared he had lost them in the house. Just as I began to worry I was going to have to find my way back into the cottage, I spotted the folder lying close to the hole. I snatched it up and stuck it in my pocket, suddenly eager to get back to my car. I was overwhelmed by the feeling that I was being watched, a feeling that wasn't uncommon for me, especially after my previous experiences with Isabella haunting me. I looked up at the house, expecting to see the little girl standing in the window but the house was still and silent.

Turning my back on the woods, I moved as quickly as I could in the direction of my car but I was distracted when I heard the sound of voices. I ducked behind the bank of rose bushes that separated the front yard from the back and peeked through to the front of the house where I caught a glimpse of a dark colored sedan parked on the lawn. It looked an awful lot like Chris Benson's unmarked detective car. I started to rise, thinking maybe he was looking for me, but then I caught a flash of clothing in the woods. I focused hard on the patch of color amidst the trees and realized that it was Chris dressed in jeans and a bright yellow polo shirt and he was talking to someone. The other man had his back to me so all I could see clearly was his height and build, taller than Chris but with the same broad shoulders and sandy blond hair. The man could easily have been related to Chris.

I watched for a moment more, unable to decipher actual words, but I got the sense that it was not a friendly conversation they were having. Chris's face was red and he seemed to be working very hard at getting words out. The other man didn't seem very concerned though. He just kept shrugging which seemed to be making Chris even angrier. Finally Chris reached out and shoved the other man. I was so surprised by the physical escalation that I stood up abruptly, putting too much weight on my right foot, causing me to tip over and crash to the ground with a cry. The pain that radiated up my leg was almost unbearable, but I tried to roll onto my knees so I could crawl back to the shelter of the rose bushes. My fall had landed me square in the middle of the yard, right in Chris's line of sight. And I had definitely been loud enough to attract the attention of both men.

Before I could pull myself to safety I heard the crunch of footsteps coming toward me from the woods. Blood was rushing into my ears and I was beginning to feel the pain crowding my senses. In that moment I felt certain that I was about to pass out from a dangerous cocktail of pain and fear, but before my conscious mind could give in to the urge to black out, a shadow enveloped me and the two men were standing over me.

"Abby?" Chris sounded genuinely surprised to have found me there. "What are you doing? Are you alright?"

The other man stared at Chris with a look of pure disgust on his face. "Are you kidding me?" he growled.

I looked up to see that the bigger man not only had a similar build and hair color, but he also had Chris's blue eyes and high cheekbones. His nose was a bit different; it looked like it had been broken at least once, maybe even twice, but there was no doubt that this man was somehow related to Chris.

He pointed at me and began yelling at Chris. "She's probably been out here the whole time! She probably heard every word we said!"

The anger dissipated from Chris's face. Now he just looked scared. "Come on Michael. You're overreacting. There's no way she heard us from all the way over here."

"Stop being stupid just because you're hung up on this girl. She's a problem. She has been a problem ever since the day she and her friend first showed up here. It's time to take care of it." The bigger man, whose name was apparently Michael, reached up and wiped beads of sweat off his forehead, then wiped the back of his hand on his t-shirt. "I'm tired of wondering just how much she knows. I'm getting rid of her."

Chris stepped forward and grabbed Michael's arm, shaking it roughly as if to snap the bigger man out of his rant. "No. No Michael. She doesn't know anything. Don't even think about it."

"She saw the footprint asshole. She knows."

"She doesn't know whose footprint it is!" Chris's voice was getting louder, his eyes wider as he tightened his grip on Michael's arm. "Abby doesn't know anything and if you touch her..."

"If I touch her what? What are you going to do? Arrest your own brother?"

I felt my mouth sag open and I looked up at the two men who were standing over me, arguing about "getting rid of me". This beast was Chris's brother?

Chris didn't answer his brother which seemed to be all the impetus he needed to bend down and sling his arm under my chest and sling me over his shoulder, my feet dangling over his back and my face buried in his armpit. Pain rocketed up my leg and I cried out but the agony of my leg being jostled so roughly rendered me motionless. I couldn't even fight Michael.

Michael turned and headed for the house. Because he had reacted so quickly Chris was a few steps behind, trying desperately to close the gap between himself and his brother who took much longer strides and was now fueled by the need to get me out of the picture. Michael carried me around the corner of the house to a small red door I hadn't know existed and ripped it open, ducking inside and yanking the door closed, locking it behind him. Moments later Chris was yanking and pounding on the door but apparently the lock was strong enough to keep him from getting it open and Michael continued to carry me through the house and into the living room where the basement door hung open.

"I can't believe he was going to sit there and do nothing about you. I told him not to spend time with you, but no. He said it wouldn't be a problem, but of course it's a goddamned problem now!" Michael's arms were shaking with anger as he descended the stairs into the basement. I could no longer hear whether or not Chris was still trying to get into the house, not that it mattered because certainly blood was thicker than water. There was no way he would go up against his brother in order to save me. From the sound of it he had already gone to fairly great lengths to keep me from connecting his brother to this house, and now I assumed to the Hollings girl's kidnapping.

I couldn't see where Michael was going but I had a feeling he was heading for the tunnel. He had stopped and seemed to be working at a door and I assumed there was a second entrance to the tunnel that Luke and I had not found, since the door we had used was now covered in a ton of debris. Michael finally got the door open and ducked inside, then closed the door behind him, throwing us into blackness. I waited a moment for my eyes to adjust as Michael fumbled for something. He must have been reaching for a flashlight because my eyes were suddenly assaulted by the bright white light of an LED light bulb. Because of the way he was carrying me the only way I could look was down and I could see the hard packed floor of the tunnel below Michael's feet.

So this was it for me. I was going to my maker in a cold, damp tunnel underneath a house I had thought was just another interesting explore. All I could think was, if only I had stayed away from exploring. If only I had remained indifferent to the hobby and just taken up scrapbooking or knitting. I tried to distract myself by counting the number of steps Michael was taking, deeper and deeper into the tunnel, but I kept getting distracted by thoughts of Nicole Hollings and how it must have felt for her, a little girl who had no understanding of what was happening to her, as she too was carried into this tunnel as I was now thoroughly convinced this was where he had taken her to die as well. I couldn't even imagine how frightened she must have been. Not that I wasn't frightened as well, but I was also forcing myself to think rationally about that fear as I was carried farther and farther down the tunnel. I thought about the woods above me, the houses full of people who had no idea that, right at that very moment, someone's life was about to end just below their feet as they went about their daily lives.

Finally I stopped trying to distract myself and closed my eyes. There was little else I could do so I turned off my mind and waited.

Chapter 21

Chris wasted a good fifteen minutes trying to pry the board off of one of the first floor windows of the cottage. He didn't know about the pantry window in the back, the one with the board that would swing to the side because all the other screws had been removed, so he had gone all the way around to the living room at the front of the house. He didn't care who saw him trying to break into the house. He just knew he had to get inside before his brother did to Abby what he was certain had already been done to little Nicole Hollings.

The board was so old and rotted that every time Chris pulled on it, it did nothing but splinter and peel. He worked at the shreds of plywood until his hands were streaked with blood and riddled with splinters, but finally it groaned and gave way, the last of the wood peeling away from the window. Bending down, he picked up a large rock and stood back to throw it through the glass, then used a stick to clear away the shards that were left so he could hoist himself over the sill.

Once inside Chris headed straight for the open basement door and down the stairs. He ran around the cellar searching frantically for the entrance to the tunnel but couldn't find any sign that there was an entrance down here. He let out a frustrated howl and pounded his already bloody fist against the nearest wall, then ran for the stairs, up and back out the living room window. Running for the yard, Chris knew his only other option was the crater in the backyard that would drop him right into the tunnel. The only question was, how far behind his brother would he be now? Michael not only had a head start, but he also knew the tunnel like the back of his hand.

Chris lowered himself into the hole and tried not to think about his leg bones splintering on impact. Thankfully the drop wasn't nearly as long as his mind imagined it to be and he landed with little more than a good solid thump as he bent his knees to absorb the impact of his feet on the hard packed earth. Now to figure out which direction his brother had gone in as he knew that somewhere up ahead the tunnel branched in three different directions. The main artery continued straight towards the Quabbin. One side branched left, running almost parallel to Blackbird Road all the way to its end. The other side took a sharp right, heading away from the tiny neighborhood enclave and back towards Route 2. He could only guess at which way his brother had gone until he heard a piercing scream coming from the main branch of the tunnel.

Funny. The scream sounded a lot like his brother…

Chapter 22

The moment I stopped trying to distract myself was the moment that Michael screamed and loosened his grip on me. Instinct kicked in and I started to squirm with every bit of energy I had left, and though it wasn't much it proved to be just enough to get him to drop me. I looked up to see what had made him scream and there, right in front of me, was the little girl I had come to know as Anne.

She appeared as a child that looked so real yet, at the same time, stunningly ethereal. She glowed with a white hot intensity that radiated anger and hate, her eyes following Michael's every move. He had stumbled as he dropped me and he was on the floor, trying to prop himself up on one knee, struggling to keep himself from looking up at Anne's translucent figure.

I too was on my knees, the pain in my ankle forgotten as the need for self preservation overwhelmed me and I crawled away, tucking myself into a tiny alcove cut into the wall of the tunnel. I watched as Michael planted his hands on his knee, trying to push himself up, but each time he did, Anne's eyes narrowed to tiny black slits and Michael cried out, dropping back down to one knee. It seemed she was somehow keeping him from regaining his equilibrium. I watched, fascinated, as she crippled him with a look that eventually drove him to flatten himself on the floor, tears pouring down his cheeks.

A moment later I heard a crashing noise in the tunnel, footsteps pounding the dust, heading in our direction. I looked over my shoulder in time to see Chris hurtling down the tunnel, ready to tackle his brother, but he stopped short as he caught sight of little Anne. He stood, transfixed, watching the tiny spirit crush his brother with her unseen gravity.

Chris seemed not to notice that I was still there, but Anne saw me. She glanced at me quickly, then back to Michael, then up at Chris. She raised her skinny white hand and pointed at Chris, then pantomimed the action of placing handcuffs on her tiny arms. Chris's mouth hung open; he didn't move, as if he didn't understand what Anne was trying to show him, but I certainly understood. Chris's handcuffs were hanging out of the back pocket of his jeans. I would never know if he had stopped to get them out of his car or if he had anticipated a confrontation with his brother long before their face to face in the woods, but that didn't matter.

I stood, wobbly but determined, and lunged for Chris's cuffs. In a serendipitous ballet of clumsiness I overshot my mark, but still managed to snag the cuffs as I fell, landing squarely on Michael's back. My legs kicked out and hooked Chris in the knees, knocking him to the ground as well. I regained my senses and slapped the handcuffs on Michael's arms, looking over my shoulder as well to see that Chris had blacked out, presumably after hitting his head on the ground.

Anne looked down at me and waited for me to make eye contact with her. When I finally did, she nodded, then gestured for me to come with her. I tried to get up but the adrenaline had finally worn off and the pain had returned. I couldn't stand. I shook my head at Anne and winced, the grimace on my face communicating to her exactly what I was feeling. She frowned, obviously disappointed that I couldn't stand.

"I can't. I can't get back up. My foot..."

Anne nodded again. Then she came around to my right side and signaled that I should sit. Dropping to the floor, I wrapped my arms under my knees and tried not to think about how badly I was hurt. Anne squatted in front of me and smoothed her white dress over her own knees, then rubbed her hands together as if she was warming her palms. She then flexed her fingers, reaching out and putting her hands on my ankle. I couldn't feel her actual touch but I could feel a sort of heat suddenly radiate through my bones, a heat that seemed to immediately eclipse the pain that I was feeling. She repeated the gesture a number of times—rub, flex, touch; rub, flex, touch—until she looked up at me and nodded with apparent satisfaction.

I got to my knees and slowly pushed myself up onto my feet. Again Anne gestured for me to follow her and she headed off down the tunnel. Just like with Isabella's spirit, it never really occurred to me to be frightened of Anne, even though most every other human being would be scared senseless, much like Michael had been when Anne appeared in front of him.

It had taken a lot of soul searching after discovering Isabella's murder to come to terms with the fact that I could see things most others couldn't. Isabella hadn't meant me any harm, nor did little Anne. There was something inside me that called to them and let them know that I was someone who could understand them and help them, and so they chose to seek me out. I supposed I would never know why that was or how it happened, but I had worked hard in the months after Westwood Asylum burned to the ground, convincing myself that my ability to see these apparitions was something of a gift.

The only thing I still wrestled with was the fact that very often this gift was coupled with devastation, loss, and death in the here and now. It wasn't just a communication with someone who had passed years ago. It seemed that every communication with one of these spirits would lead to a shift in circumstances, often ending in death, whether it happened to be suicide or murder. Cameron's suicide had been a direct result of my delving into a decades old murder. Nicole Hollings had been kidnapped and I was certain that little Anne was now leading me to yet another dead child. That part of the equation would never cease to pain me.

I followed Anne down the tunnel until she stopped in front of another wooden door.
"Should I open it?"

Anne nodded.

"Am I going to be sad if I look behind that door?"

Anne shook her head, then smiled at me. She took a deep breath in, then closed her eyes as if she was concentrating deeply.

"She's still alive," she whispered. It was the same whisper I had heard in my dream.

It took a moment for her words to sink in, but the moment they did, I threw myself at the door, yelling Nicole's name and clawing at the door to get it open, but it didn't budge. I backed up and slammed my shoulder into the door over and over until I finally heard it splinter under my weight. I kept hitting it until the wood shattered and I found myself on the other side, in a tiny room where Nicole Hollings sat, curled in a ball on a ratty old mattress. She was dirty and bruised, blood crusted on her nose and lips, one eye swollen shut, but she was alive.

"Nicole, honey, my name is Abby. I'm going to get you out of here."

The child looked up, terror shining in her one good eye, which was bloodshot from lack of sleep and constant fear. I could see that she was trembling.

For a moment she stared as if she hadn't understood what I was saying to her, but then she nodded and held out her arms to be picked up, melting my heart instantly. I bent and lifted her up, oblivious to the sudden extra weight of holding a ten year old in my arms, and I stumbled out into the tunnel. I had no idea which way was out and Anne was nowhere to be found. In the midst of all the chaos a moment ago she had disappeared, most likely with the understanding that her presence would only serve to frighten Nicole even more. I knew I had to head back the way I had come, but once I reached the spot where I had handcuffed Michael and knocked Chris unconscious I would be lost.

I started off into the darkness, Nicole clinging to me like a spider monkey, until I caught sight of Chris standing over his brother who was still cuffed, but was no sitting up against the wall of the tunnel. Chris stepped out in front of me with his hands outstretched in a gesture of both surrender and welcome, as if he was reaching out to hold me.

"Abby, thank God! I didn't know where you'd gone and I..."

I brushed past him roughly, turning my body away from him so that he couldn't reach for Nicole. "Save it Chris. I heard everything you and your brother said to each other. You knew all along that he had kidnapped this little girl and you did nothing!"

"Abby wait!" Chris reached out for my arm but I twisted away, lengthening my strides and moving as quickly as I could. The only problem was that I was no completely lost. As I moved though, I felt as if I was being pushed down the tunnel. I turned to see who or what was pushing me but I could see no one. Then I looked a bit closer. Tiny footprints had appeared in the dust behind me. Anne was there, guiding me out of the tunnel.

Anne pushed me down the tunnel through a number of lefts and rights, guiding me out of the tunnel with Chris right on my heels. I started to run as quickly as I could with Nicole in my arms, her face buried in my neck. I knew she was terrified but she was being so brave and holding on so tight. I turned to see Chris pursuing us but he was moving slowly, his hand to his head. He must have hit it harder then I suspected, but it meant that with Anne's help I might make it to the yard before he did.

Fearing Chris might regain his senses at any moment and close the gap between us, I pushed myself to move faster until I felt Anne directing me to a small corridor to the right which branched off the main tunnel. At the end of the little hallway I could see a breath of sunlight sneaking through wooden slats. It was a door and safety was just beyond it.

"Hang on Nicole, we're almost out of here but I need to put you down for a minute." The little girl protested for a moment, then allowed me to put her down so that I could work at opening the door. She clung to my hip, hiding her face in my shirt. "Dammit. The door is locked." I worked at the handle until I was sweating, but it was clear it wasn't going to budge. "I'm going to have to break it."

I bent down and put my hands on Nicole's shoulders, forcing her to look at me. "Sweetie, I'm going to have to break the door. It's going to be loud but I don't want you to be scared."

The little girl nodded and stuck a grimy thumb in her mouth. I looked around and spied another alcove in the wall behind her. "Hide in here. Put your hands over your ears if you have to." I pushed her into the cubby and watched her cover her ears, but she kept her eyes open and trained on the darkness in the main tunnel.

I turned my attention back to the door and tried to figure out the best way to force it open. Finally I turned my shoulder to the door and threw my weight against it. It vibrated a bit under my body, but not enough to shake it loose. I tried again, this time putting even more momentum behind the hit. The door was old and strong, but I was determined to get through and get out. Just as I was about to put my shoulder into it one more time Chris came skidding around the corner.

I made eye contact with him and felt my blood boil, a surge of adrenaline pulsing through my veins. I looked away from him and launched myself against the door again. Suddenly I was stumbling, flying through space only to land on the dirt floor of the basement under the cottage. I looked up to see that the door had been hidden by a workbench bolted to the wall with shelves above it. No one would have ever known that there was a door behind it. The sunlight was streaming in through a hole in the foundation.

Ducking back into the hallway I put both my hands out in front of me like battering rams and hit Chris hard in the chest, sending him flying for the second time. It gave me just long enough to grab Nicole from her hiding place and make a mad dash for the stairs that would take us up and out of the house. I found the shattered living room window and lifted Nicole through it, placing her carefully on her feet on the front lawn.

"Abby! Look out!" Nicole had raised her finger to point over my shoulder but her warning was a moment too late. Michael had come to and was standing behind me, his hands still cuffed in front of him. He must have stepped over his hands in order to untangle himself from the cuffs. He had a lamp in his hand and had raised it over his head. I closed my eyes, knowing there was no way I could get away from him fast enough.

"Run Nicole! Run home to your parents!"

The little girl hesitated a moment, then turned and ran in the direction of her house. At least she would get home safely and her parents could call the police. I held my breath and waited for the blow to come, but instead I was deafened by the sound of a gunshot, followed by the sound of my own scream. I opened my eyes just enough to see Michael lying on the ground, Chris standing over him with his service revolver still drawn, the barrel smoking. The image was then replaced by blackness. Complete and utter blackness.

Chapter 23

I came to out on the front lawn, a paramedic bending over me, checking for injuries. "I'm fine. I just passed out." I struggled to sit up, my head still spinning from both the sound of the gunshot ringing in my ears and the tide of blackness that still hovered at the edge of my consciousness. A wave of nausea and dizziness crept up and I breathed deep, willing it to pass. "Where is Nicole?"

The paramedic pointed to a cavalcade of cruisers parked on the grass where Nicole Hollings was clinging to a woman I could only assume was her mother. The little girl looked up and caught my eye, letting go of her mother and rushing over to me. She threw herself into my arms and hugged me tight around the neck.

"Thank you!" she whispered. "And tell Anne I said thank you too for keeping me company."

She scampered off and rejoined her parents, an ambulance waiting to take her to the hospital for a once over. A moment later it registered what she had said and I stood, closing my eyes as a head rush threatened to overtake me, and ran over to Nicole.

"Wait, you saw Anne?" I asked, squatting down with my hands on Nicole's shoulders. The girl nodded and smiled.

"She came to see me every night and told me that I was going to be ok because you were going to come for me."

I was dumbfounded. Not only had she seen Anne, but Anne had spoken to her. Most amazing of all was that Nicole wasn't the least bit frightened by the fact that a tiny spirit girl had visited her on a nightly basis while she was being held captive by a murderer. Anne had kept Nicole from giving up the entire time she had been hidden away in the tunnel.

"Is that the first time you've seen someone like Anne?"

Smiling, Nicole shook her head, her greasy little pigtails sweeping side to side with the motion. "My kitty, Norman, died once and he comes to sleep with me sometimes. And my Nana. She comes to visit too. It's nice. I like when they visit."

Amazing. This little girl was just like me. "Nicole, don't ever turn them away. Even if what they have to say is scary. Promise?"

"I promise." She held up her little pinky finger, waiting for me to link mine with hers, proof of her promise. We pinky swore and I hugged her one more time, the paramedics beginning to look impatient to whisk her away.

As they bundled Nicole into the ambulance her parents turned to me, tears of relief and gratitude in their eyes. Her mother, choking on tears as she searched for words, reached out for my hands and held them tight. "Thank you so much for giving her back to us."

Her husband, whose name I remembered was Jim, put his arm around his wife. Obviously a man of lesser words, he nodded his thanks and gently tugged on his wife's shoulder. She squeezed my hands quickly, then turned and headed for the ambulance. As they pulled away, lights flashing but the siren quiet, I looked over at the cruisers gathered in front of me and watched as a stern faced man in a suit relieved Detective Chris Benson of his gun and badge. A uniformed officer stepped behind Chris and clapped on a pair of handcuffs.

Walking over to Chris, I felt a momentary surge of pity for the man who had tried so hard to protect his older brother. He had given up everything, ruined his own life, to hide a monster in plain sight. I stepped in front of him and stared at his face, wondering how he could have allowed Nicole Hollings to suffer the way she did. Then I wondered how many others there were. How many times had his brother gotten away with kidnapping and torturing children? The pity disappeared and before I knew it I felt myself lift my hand and slap Chris across the face. A few of the officers started forward but the man in the suit shook his head as if to tell them to back off.

Chris hung his head, my handprint clearly visible on his cheek. "Abby, I don't know what to say."

I took a deep breath and narrowed my eyes, a feeble attempt at controlling the anger that welled up inside me. "There is absolutely nothing in the world that you could possibly say. You lied to me. You lied to your department. You lied to that girl's parents! You told them she was dead! And then you went on living your life as if she was! What were you going to do? Wait until your brother killed her? And then what? Were you going to dump the body somewhere and make it look like someone else killed her?"

Chris said nothing, though I waited a few long minutes for his reply.

I shook my head in disgust. "That's exactly what you were going to do. You planned to cover up a child's murder in order to save your brother's ass. You're despicable. I hope they lock you away for a very long time."

Turning, I nodded to the officers, then walked away, heading back to my car. I heard one of the uniforms begin to read Chris his rights, then listened for the slamming car door. As I walked across the street to my car parked in the layby, I kept my head down and the cruisers passed me, one by one. I never looked up. I didn't want to see Chris Benson's face ever again.

Chapter 24

Months later Chris Benson was brought to trial for everything he had done to cover for his brother. The papers reported that he was considered an accessory to the kidnapping of Nicole

Hollings and was charged as such. The police also discovered that he had covered up a number of assaults and attempted kidnappings over a span of almost twenty years, a cycle that began long before Chris had joined the force. I learned from the news articles that Chris had become a cop simply to protect his brother. He said in court that he had always wanted to be a writer. Well, he would have a hell of a memoir to publish now.

I too had a hell of a story to tell. I had unwittingly walked into what could have been the horrible murder of a child. This time I had been lucky and death had not followed me. Instead I had helped save the life of a little girl. According to those same news reporters, I was a hero.

Thankfully I was not called upon to testify in court. The police had searched the homes of both brothers and uncovered enough evidence to convict Chris without my testimony. I was spared the agony of reliving the entire nightmare. Nicole did not have to testify either, though her parents were in the courtroom gallery every day until the moment Chris Benson was sentenced to twenty five years in prison. Parole was not discussed.

Nicole Hollings returned to her home a remarkably well adjusted little girl in spite of everything that had happened. She never told her parents about Anne; I'm certain she sensed that they wouldn't quite understand about the spirit girl who had helped her through her ordeal. She did, however, talk to me about it quite a bit.

A few weeks after the court case was settled I went back to the Murray Farm for the first time since I had pulled Nicole from that tunnel. The crime scene tape was gone and the house seemed remarkably sunny and quiet given its gruesome history. The police had discovered the box of murder trophies that Chris Benson had concealed. It turned out that along with my own prints as well as Luke's, the box held the fingerprints of Chris, Michael, *and* the man who had killed the first group of girls back in the 1970's.

Unfortunately there was no chance that the killer would be brought to justice; he had died in a car accident in the early 1980's. His name was Joshua Deering, a young man who had lived in the Murray cottage as a hired hand, and who had never been considered a suspect because he had had an alibi for the murder of Evelyn Burrows, the first child to go missing from the neighborhood. Anne was his final victim.

While the front of the cottage looked as it did the first time I had seen it, the backyard of the Murray Farm was completely cordoned off. Police had descended on the property with cadaver dogs and mobile crime scene units. They dug up the yard, the tunnels, and the basement, eventually finding the bodies of all thirteen girls buried in various locations. Little Anne had been buried under the floor in the room where Michael had held Nicole Hollings captive. The families of the girls were notified and each one given a proper burial. I attended Anne's burial and though I couldn't be certain, I thought I saw her peeking around a tree, watching the proceedings with something resembling delight.

As I stared at the chaos in the backyard of the Murray Farm, I felt a tiny hand slip into mine and I looked down to see Nicole beaming up at me.

"Hey kiddo." I lowered myself to the lawn and Nicole immediately crawled into my lap, putting her arms around my neck and hugging me.

"Hi Abby. My mom said she saw your car here and said I could come see you."

I smiled and hugged Nicole back. "I'm glad you did."

"Why did you come here?"

"I just wanted to see it," I said quietly. "So I wouldn't be afraid of it anymore. Are you afraid of it?"

Nicole shook her head. "Nope. That man is gone and they found all those little girls. The house is empty now."

"What do you mean empty?"

She shrugged as if the answer should have been obvious to me. "They all went home."

36261754R00076

Made in the USA
San Bernardino, CA
18 July 2016